THE MANSION MYSTERY

by AMIT RAY

Illustrated by: Tamara Antonijevic
Cover design: Tamara Antonijevic
Edited by: Light Hurley

www.theraywriter.com

Dedication

To Sid, for whom I made up this story,
And Sandhya, who (mostly) made Sid,
You expected a masterpiece of glory,
But this is all I did.

Acknowledgements

I blame my brother, Sumit, and cousin, Anasuya, for being strange children. If you'd been normal, none of this would have happened.

My parents and relatives aren't much better. No point denying it, Ray's and Ghosh's. Meshouncle, your horse paintings do seem to be on the verge of pooping but, I must say, they look magnificent doing so. And Mashimuni, let me place on record that I never enjoyed the bitter gourd.

Then we have the accessories to this crime: Sandhya, my wife, and Sid, my son. They had opportunities to stop this travesty at draft stage but egged me on with encouragements like "When do you start your next job again?" and "Please don't make my friends read this."

"But Amit," you may well ask, "Why didn't you get a professional to edit this drivel?"

To which I would say, "Alas, I did."

The so-called professional in question, Light Hurley, should have lightly hurled the manuscript into a fireplace. Instead, the lure of lucre caused him to abandon his principles and focus on salvaging rather than savaging the book.

And let us not forget Tamara Antonijevic, who deserves her share of the blame for distracting you with her beautiful illustrations. If it weren't for her, you'd know how bad the story telling really is.

All their bad judgment was thankfully negated by my diligent previewers, who sacrificed holiday time to save their fellow children from my poor taste. They made this book bearable with feedback on content and pacing and by highlighting things that were hard to understand. Thank you Savitur Swarup, Ayan Dalmia, Aanya Pandey, Ishani Chaudhuri, Naomi D'Silva, Siddharth Ray, Arjun K Bharadwaj, Yatharth and Parth Shukla, Mrityunjay Sethi, Krish Palod, Vito Suarez, Yash Bambawale, and Akhil Thomas. You rock!

Contents

CHAPTER 1

A Ball Is Lost

"I'm bored," said Neel, lying spread-eagled on the floor in his thin cotton vest. "And hot. Bored and hot. Hot and bored. Hotenboard, hotenboard, hotenboard."

Like all Kolkata summer days, today was sweltering hot. The whirring of the vintage ceiling fan did little more than lull the family into their holiday siesta. Ma was sleeping on the massive teak bed, Didu on her right, and Nick was hanging off the left reading Anna's old X-men comic.

"Why are we always in Kolkata?" piped up Neel. "Your friend, Shivalik, went to London with his parents. He's probably watching London Bridge falling down right now. Not like here, not like in Maharaja Nandakumar Road. Nothing's falling down here. Nothing other than bits of our balcony. And that's just not the same."

The sprawling old mansion they lived in had a name, Prosadi, after Ram Prasad Sen, himself an ancestor of the family and eighteenth-century saint. The family home had been originally built in 1936 amongst the thickets of South Kolkata. It had housed the family of Manas Ranjan Sen, which included his four sons, their wives and children, and of course their staff. Eighty years later, it now stood dilapidated, the thickets long cut away for the sprawling city, its gates signposted by a garbage dump.

Moss had been growing up the underside of the filigree balconies for years. Just the other day, a piece of plaster had fallen from one, giving a passing hawker a nasty fright. Neel, who had the misfortune of being on the balcony at the time, had faced the brunt of the man's ire.

Nick looked away from his younger brother and flipped to the next page; Magneto, Professor X's arch enemy, was about to hatch a plot and there was always the chance that if Nick ignored Neel long enough he'd fall asleep or fall silent.

"... Nick?"

...

"Nick?"

...

"Nikki!"

"What! What!" said Nick, slamming shut the comic and sitting up to look at Neel. "What's the matter with you? Yes, it's hot. It's summer. It's hot every day!"

"I'm bored," said Neel. "Let's do something."

Nick stole a glance at the X-Men. Who knew when his cousin Anna would wake up and demand her comic back? She was pretty possessive about her things.

"You know we aren't allowed to play with the iPad in the afternoon. Do you want to play Snakes and Ladders maybe?" asked Nick.

"Umm... no."

Neel wasn't fond of Snakes and Ladders. He never won. He landed on every snake and almost never got a ladder. And when he got a ladder he'd always get the very next snake. And if he somehow scraped his way to the end he'd find his way right to square 98, the lair of the longest, most horrible snake, which would send him all the way back to 16.

"Chess?"

Chess was way worse. Not only would he lose, it would only take about a minute to do so. That wouldn't exactly help kill time.

"How about cricket?" suggested Neel.

"Cricket? We'd wake the whole house!" said Nick, shaking his head. "Don't you have any sense? Why don't we just play football in the bedroom then? Ma and Didu can be the goalposts!"

"Obviously not in the corridor," said Neel patiently. "Upstairs. On the terrace."

"But it's like two in the afternoon!"

"So?"

"If you're hot down here, you'll be baking on the terrace! And the roof will be too hot to even step on."

"It's okay," said Neel, enthusiastically. At least Nick was discussing the idea, which was a good sign. "We'll wear our slippers, and there's a bit of a breeze outside. Come on, it'll be fun."

Without waiting for an answer, Neel dashed out of the room and up the stairs to the terrace.

Nick stood still for a second, then, with a sigh, put on his slippers and followed Neel. It was no use arguing with his headstrong brother. Perhaps the afternoon sun would convince him to return downstairs soon, but he held little hope.

He took the stairs out onto a short, covered landing. On the left was a pair of attic rooms, on the right an open terrace. One of the rooms was used by their uncle as a painting studio and both Nick and Neel - especially Neel - had been forbidden from entering it without adult supervision. It was latched at the moment, since their uncle was taking a nap. He would probably be back in the evening to continue work on his latest masterpiece; a horse that looked like it was about to take a very satisfying poop.

The other room was always locked. Every summer Nick and Neel would peek through its dusty glass, but all they had ever been able to make out was a mess of furniture that never changed. It was probably a storeroom for old stuff. In front of it was a corner with a tap and a drain that was used for washing utensils. Such a washing area was common in old houses, dating from a time when people didn't want unwashed vessels to touch anything else. Now, the washing area was being used to store some gigantic, old urns that didn't fit any of the newer kitchen cabinets.

Blinking in the afternoon glare, Nick emerged onto the terrace to find Neel already in possession of the little wooden bat and ball. Usually they were kept in the corner. Both pieces of equipment looked almost as ancient as the house.

The bat had originally belonged to Anna. Neel, recognizing its potential as a weapon of destruction, had claimed it almost as soon as he could walk. It had worn over the years, partly because Neel often used it to hammer and pound things, and also because he would sportingly fling the bat on the ground, and occasionally at Nick, whenever he celebrated losing at cricket.

The ball was even older. It had once served as the plaything of the family dog who had made it his life's purpose to separate the ball from its covering, chewing and slobbering his way to success over many years. All that was left was a few wisps of felt across the smooth rubber surface. It was a wonder it still bounced!

The terrace was their stadium. A line of bricks neatly divided the space in two, marking out a net for badminton tournaments, and discarded flowerpots were often repurposed as goalposts for impromptu football games. Half the terrace was also the perfect size for a two-person game of dodge ball or *langri*, a version of tag where the tagger could only hop on one leg.

But the real treasure was the rusty water tank that stood proudly near one end of the terrace. Though it no longer held any water, it was positioned perfectly where the wickets should be. Some enterprising school kid, possibly one of Anna's friends, had scratched the outline of wickets on its side, and this is where Neel had taken up his position.

"Here, catch!" said Neel, claiming first right to bat.

Nick took his position at the line of bricks, which, among its many uses, also served as the bowling crease. Keeping in mind that Neel's sporting prowess was more imagination than talent, Nick bowled a slow, straight ball as his first delivery. Neel swung hard, clipping the edge of the bat and sending the ball spinning into the tank behind.

"What are you doing?" yelled Nick. "Hit the ball gently! Last time you made me go down to the street four times. I'm not going down to get it again."

"Okay, sorry, sorry! I'll just block the ball next time, okay?"

Ball two - slow and straight again. Neel connected better this time. It bounced along the ground to the wall for four runs.

"Yay! Four runs, four runs, four runs..." chanted Neel, skipping back to the batting position.

Nick sighed in relief. Now that Neel had scored, he would have less to grumble about when he got out. He started bowling a little faster, aiming directly at the wicket in the hope that Neel would swing and miss.

Neel was high on confidence, however, and played a crafty innings, doing just enough to deflect the ball away from Nick and steal a few runs while Nick scrambled to collect the ball.

After about a dozen balls, Nick was getting cross. The afternoon sun was really beating down on him and Neel was proving to be more trouble than expected. Worse, every time Neel scored any runs, he'd dance the floss, turning around and shaking his butt at Nick. He was definitely trying to get under Nick's skin. It was time to raise things a notch with a bit of spin bowling.

The next ball he bowled was a spinner that cut across Neel's body and caught him completely by surprise. Neel jabbed at it wildly, but missed. It thudded right next to the outline of the wicket.

"Ooh!" went Nick. It had been so close!

Nick quickly gathered the ball and threw in his next delivery, a sharp off-spin that dropped towards Neel's right and cut inwards. This time he did not miss. *Whump*, the ball went, right into the middle of the wicket.

"Out!" yelled Nick. "You're out."

Neel looked for a moment as if he were about to contest the decision, but gave in. Nick grabbed the bat out of Neel's hands and dashed to the wicket.

This had worked out better than he thought. Now he could quickly score his runs and get back downstairs with enough time to try and finish his X-Men comic.

Being smaller than Nick, Neel was allowed to throw the ball from over his shoulder rather than bowling underarm. It didn't help much though. Neel's first delivery was quickly knocked to the wall for four runs.

"Next," called Nick as he rushed back to his position. It would take just a few balls to cross Neel's score. Soon he'd be back in bed with his comic.

Another overarm throw, this time a juicy volley. Nick, in his excitement, hit it into the pots in the corridor. The resulting clanging was like a thunderclap in the stillness of the afternoon. He expected the entire household to come charging up at any moment. Luckily, his only audience turned out to be a rather drowsy maid, who seemed to think the mischief was due to pigeons and settled back into her siesta after a couple of incoherent threats.

"Shh!" said Neel, relishing the opportunity to put Nick on the defensive for once.

The next couple of balls were tame affairs. Nick, wary of the maid, just blocked the ball.

"You'll never beat me at this rate," mocked Neel. "Remember, you only get two overs to beat my score!"

"Two overs? Why only two overs?" asked Nick, stumped by this new rule that Neel had just made up.

"At school we allow only two overs to big boys who play small boys otherwise it's unfair," said Neel, relishing the delicious unfairness of his rule.

"I don't believe that for a second," said Nick. "Why didn't you tell me this before? Why did you make me waste two balls?"

"I did tell you. I'm telling you now. I could've told you after two overs, right?" said Neel. "I'm being fair. More than fair. You should thank me!"

"Come here so I can thank you with this bat!" roared Nick, as Neel skipped away to the head of the stairs.

Nick took a threatening step towards him.

"I'll tell Ma," said Neel gaily, as he retreated a couple of steps down the staircase.

Defeated, Nick walked back to the crease. "Okay, fine. Let's play."

The next ball was a slow one that Nick knocked towards the terrace wall for four runs. Unfortunately, it took an odd bounce right at the end and sailed over the edge of the roof. They heard it thudding on the street below.

"Who did this? Whose ball is this?" yelled someone who had clearly had better mornings.

Neel stopped dead in his tracks.

"Nick, go on. Have a look!" he said.

"Yeah, sure. Okay," said Nick, willing his leaden legs to move towards the terrace wall. He peeped over.

A cotton seller had stopped squarely in the middle of the road and was darting menacing looks across the rooftops. On his shoulder was his cotton-fluffer, looking like a particularly vicious machine gun. At the back of his cycle was a gigantic sack of fluffy, milky-white cotton. And nestled right in the middle of the sack like some sort of gangrenous pustule was their dog-bitten, germ-infested ball with streaks of a tarry black residue marking the path it had made across the pristine white bed.

"S-sorry Mister. I'm, I'm coming down," quavered Nick, his face rapidly taking on the color of the cotton.

"Is this yours?" the cotton-seller asked, waving the ball at Nick as he stepped out onto the street.

All Nick could do in response was to stare at the man's slippers. Neel, meanwhile, sticking to Nick's backside like a barnacle, was letting out wisps of sound like steam escaping a kettle.

"Sss-sss-ss-ss-ss," he went, burying his face in Nick's t-shirt to try and muffle his laughter. "Nick... ss-ss-ss... his face is... ss-ss-ss... so purple... ss-ss-ss-

ss… like an... ss-ss-ss... eggplant sssss-ss-ss-ss-ss-ss."

"Well, is it?" the man demanded.

"Yes," said Nick in an uncharacteristically small voice.

"Why is it in my cotton?" The man's voice was growing louder and his face taking on a darker shade. Nick really wished he were somewhere else.

"We… we were playing cricket and-"

"Do you think it's a - a cotton ball?" the man roared.

This was too much for Neel. "Sss-sss-sss," he went, now wiping tears of delight onto Nick's back.

"Who's that?" the man huffed.

Neel peeked out at the man. One look at his tear-streaked face and the man's anger evaporated.

"Oh, oh, oh, little boy, don't cry. Don't cry, please! I was only trying to tell you boys to be more careful. Oh no, what is all this? Please don't cry."

He looked about hastily, hoping their parents weren't anywhere around.

"Here you are," said the cotton-seller, tossing the ball to Nick and starting down the road. "Be more careful next time. You might hurt someone."

The cotton-seller pedaled away, leaving Nick and Neel alone in the middle of the street.

Neel looked at Nick. "What just happened?"

"I have no idea," said Nick, gazing at the back of the cotton-seller as he went twang-twang-twang in the distance. "But I'm not waiting to find out. Let's go."

The boys ran back into the house and up the stairs. They took up their playing positions.

Nick had a choice to make. If he continued playing hard, he'd probably get into more trouble. But if Neel won, he'd spend the rest of his life telling everyone about it. All his friends would wonder how he was beaten by a chubby little seven-year-old. He'd be the last guy to be picked for teams. Like that Rinku who stood like a tree in front of the wickets wasting balls and guaranteeing defeat. No. Nick couldn't let it happen. He had win. He had to hit the ball. Even if Neel threw it right off the roof!

Meanwhile, Neel was fully charged up. Nick had to play gently now. He was no longer invincible. Victory was within his grasp. All he had to do was throw straight and hard and he would prevail over his nemesis. He could do it. He would do it.

Closing his eyes, Neel leaned back in preparation for his master delivery.

"Wakanda forever!" he yelled, lunging forward to unleash a deadly pulse of power just as Nick, eyes bulging, bat aloft, leapt forward ready to smash the ball into kingdom come.

"Mommy!" cried Neel, hastily hurling the ball in the general direction of Nick while simultaneously dashing for the safety of the staircase. His throw went wide off the mark.

Nick darted to his right, holding the bat in one hand like a tennis racket, and took a wild swipe. The ball glanced off the edge of the bat and flew up, spinning sharply towards the corridor, where it bounced off the wall and through the missing windowpane of their uncle's studio.

The boys looked at each other in horror.

CHAPTER 2

Search and Rescue

"Out," called Neel.

Nick glared at him. "No."

"That's definitely out."

"This is your fault! Why the heck were you bowling so wide?"

"But-"

"No buts! I don't want to hear anything. I don't even care about your silly game. None of this would have happened if you had just let me read my X-Men in peace. Why can't you just sleep in the afternoon like everyone else, huh? Now what do we do?"

Nick walked over to the studio and peered in through the hole. The room was dark. He couldn't see much more of it than where the shadow of his head was framed in sunlight and the latched door, but he couldn't go in.

The boys had been banned from going into the studio alone ever since Neel, then four and learning finger painting in school, had wandered into the room and put the finishing touches on a damp four-foot horse with his palm. Neel had been in the process of wiping the paint from his hands onto the walls when he had been discovered. "Good horsey," he had gurgled to Mesho as he was hastily removed from the scene.

"Nick," whispered Neel standing tiptoe by Nick's shoulder. He wasn't tall enough to look in. In fact, all he could see was a gloomy ceiling. "Can you see it?"

"No," said Nick, eyes slowly adjusting to the dim light. "I can't see it. Even if I could, I don't know how we'd get it."

"Nick, we have to. If Mesho finds the ball inside he's going to know it was us."

"You think I don't know that?" hissed Nick, glaring at Neel. He wished there were a way to yell at him without waking up the whole neighborhood.

"Maybe he'll think the ghost of the doggie has returned from the afterlife to play fetch?" said Neel. "These rooms definitely look like they might be housing a spirit or two!"

"No, he won't," replied Nick. "And you're a real nut if you think anyone is going to believe that."

"Phew, thank God. Ghosts would have been pretty scary!" Neel slid down to the floor with a sigh.

"Maybe if we-" began Nick, turning away from the window to find Neel contemplatively squatting on the ground. "For God's sake do you want to get into trouble? Get up and help me figure out what to do. If Mesho finds the ball there'll be at least two ghosts added to the house! Will you be happy then? Get up!"

Neel scrambled to his feet and dusted off his shirt and shorts. Why had he ever wanted to play cricket? Had it been worth it?

Nick paced up and down the corridor as Neel hopped up and down, trying to get a look inside.

"Lift me up so I can see," suggested Neel after a few attempts.

"Dear God, no way!" said Nick, pausing to look at the rotund figure of Neel bouncing at the window. He spotted a nearby flowerpot large enough to hold Neel.

Trrrrrrrrshhh. He dragged it up to the window, turning it over into a makeshift stool.

"Stand on this. But there's nothing to see. The ball must be in a corner or something."

Hooking his fingers onto the hollow windowpane, Neel hoisted himself up, balancing on just one foot. He brought his face close to the window and could just about make out the dim outlines of the room. There at the end was the easel, the canvas set up exactly as Mesho must have left it in the morning. Beside the easel were the chair and table, the bed. The table seemed to have some odds and ends on it, but he couldn't make them out in the gloom.

Neel turned to Nick, who was still rushing about in wound-up-tin-soldier mode.

"Nick."

He kept pacing.

"Nick!"

Nick came to a stop, staring at Neel blankly. Neel knew that look. Everyone in the family did.

"What?"

"We have to go in. What if the ball landed on the palette or knocked over some paint or something? We got to find out."

Nick watched him, and then started to look away again.

Neel sighed. "Earth to Nick... Earth to Nick!"

Nick's eyes came back to life. "What?"

"Come on. We've got no other choice."

"Hang on," said Nick. "We came up at 3 o'clock. It must be almost four by now. People have probably already started waking up. Mesho will be here soon. You know how he can't bear to be separated from his paintings. If the ball has gone into a corner or under something we might have to move things around and then put everything back. It'll take too long."

"But what if he finds it?"

"We can't see it. So the ball's well hidden. We should do it tomorrow; we'd have more time. Let's just take another peek in and then go down."

Neel liked that idea. He stepped back onto the flowerpot while Nick stood behind him. They did another quick scan of the room. Everything seemed fine.

As if on cue, they heard Ma's voice calling from the corridor below, "Nick… Neel… Where are you? Come down for your milk… Niiick… Neeeeel."

"Coming!" yelled the boys in unison.

Neel hopped off the pot and dashed down. It was snack time. There'd be samosas or mango with the milk. He didn't want to miss any of it, ball or no ball.

Nick carefully dragged the pot back to where it had been and scuffed up its reddish trail with the heel of his slippers. Then he followed Neel down the stairs. Something smelt good. No point keeping it waiting!

***

It was the next afternoon. Something was tugging at the sleeve of Nick's t-shirt.

"Wha-?" he slurred, opening his eyes a crack. A blurry, pink balloon was floating just inches away from his face. His eyes flew open and he jerked his head back.

"Wh-what?"

"Shh! C'mon!"

The world came into focus. Neel was kneeling on the floor, peering into his face.

"C'mon!" he whispered. "It's time."

Nick lay back and closed his eyes. He sighed and wagged a finger to signal that he would be up shortly.

A few moments passed as he gathered his thoughts. It was afternoon. Had he fallen asleep reading? The panicky thumping in Nick's chest had settled.

He sat up and rubbed his eyes. The book on his chest slipped to the floor and fell face down with a slap.

Nick sprang to the floor to pick it up. This was another of Anna's books, a hardcover this time, meriting even more love and care. Anna would kill him!

Luckily there was no damage. Nick hurriedly noted the page number, closed the book, and placed it carefully on the bed.

"Okay, let's go," whispered Nick and the boys crept up the stairs to the terrace.

It was almost three o'clock. Nick and Neel crept up to the studio door and peeked in through the broken pane. All was as it was. The room shrouded in darkness.

Nick slowly lifted the latch and tried to slide it open. It hadn't been oiled in years. *Squeeeeak,* it went as he jiggled it a bit. Nick dropped to a crouch. Had anyone heard? Neel was cowering on the stairs, expecting Mesho - or worse yet, Mashi - to come marching up.

Moments passed. No sounds below. Nobody stirred.

Nick gave it another try. *Squeak,* the latch went as it slid another centimeter. It was clearly not going to cooperate. He'd have to just do it.

Squeaky-squeaky-squeaky-squeak-CLACK went the latch as Nick jiggled it up and down with both hands till it slid all the way across. The boys froze again like startled rabbits, listening for the smallest indication that someone had heard. The door fell open a crack.

Nothing.

Phew.

Nick beckoned to Neel, who scampered up in a half-squat and pushed open the door to look in. It was dark inside, the afternoon sun no match for decades of dust on the windowpanes. An invisible hand seemed to hold them back.

"This is it, Nilu," said Nick, placing his hand on Neel's shoulder.

"This is it," said Neel. He squared his shoulders and plunged into the room.

Nick followed. He couldn't but help admire his plucky little brother. Neel was a real trooper!

They stood side by side in the dim light for a few moments.

Nick patted his brother on the shoulder. "We'll find it soon. Then this will all just be a bad memory."

"Can you reach the switches?" asked Neel. They were on the wall to their right, too high for Neel.

Nick could just about reach them. "Sure," he said, standing on his tiptoes. The switches were ancient, just like the rest of house. Three of them jutted out of a wooden electrical box screwed to the wall.

He flicked the first switch. Nothing.

"Nick," said Neel. "There are wires hanging out."

Nick had noticed them too. He didn't feel too excited about poking around inches of 100-year-old electrical wire patched with scotch tape. He wasn't even wearing his slippers.

It took all his courage to flip that second switch.

Wannnnnnnnnnnng... wannnnnnnng... wannnnng... wanng... wang... wang-wang-wang went something overhead.

Neel stood stock still. What was that?

"It's the fan, it's just the fan," said Nick, flicking the switch off. "At least the switches are working."

He had to stretch to reach the last switch and only reached it with the tips of his fingers. *Bzzzt.* A bulb came on, yellow light flickering like a candle before it settled into a feeble glow.

Neel looked around, forgetting for a moment the urgency of finding the ball. He had never been to this room before. Since Neel's last escapade, Mesho had shifted his studio a couple of times, from a room downstairs to another one on the same level to this latest one in the attic. He seemed to draw fresh inspiration from changing surroundings.

The room was long and narrow. On the left of the entrance was a camp bed, the collapsible kind used for guests. This one was long past its prime. Its metal frame was warped and the canvas frayed and torn. Junk was scattered across it - books, discarded bottles, art supplies. On the right was some shelving, and at the far end stood Mesho's easel, and the writing desk and chair.

Neel walked up to the easel. "Another horse," he exclaimed. "Can't he paint, like, a mountain or something? He made all these horses, then he made goats, then fishes. And do you remember when I had a nightmare about some clown he drew for my birthday? And now he's making horses again! These look like they're being tortured. Look at this one. Its head is looking at me and its body is pointing in the opposite direction. What horse can do that?"

"Who cares what you think? Mesho is a really great artist and his paintings are in museums all over the world," said Nick. "Remember that guy who came visiting the other day? He was an art collector. He said Mesho's horses are better than those by M.F. Husain or even Leonardo da Vinci!"

"Then he's a bumble head," said Neel curtly, turning to the table.

It was covered by a stained and dusty tablecloth. A flat, wooden board, which Mesho used as his palette, lay on it. It was where he mixed colors. Beside the board was an assortment of paintbrushes as well as a narrow trowel that Mesho used to dab on thick layers of paint or to scrape it off. Most of the brushes had dried and hardened. Neel knew Mesho could get them clean and soft in a jiffy with a dash of some smelly liquid he kept in a jar. Also present was a tray full of tubes of paint, looking very much like toothpaste!

"Do you see the ball by any chance?" asked Nick, poking around in a corner behind the door.

"No," said Neel turning towards Nick with a start. "It must be under something."

"You wanna take a look?" asked Nick. He was pretty sure there would be cobwebs and possibly even a spider or two. No point in two people mucking around in there.

"On it," said Neel, kneeling on the ground and poking his head under the table. The little light in the room wasn't really of much help. He'd have to crawl under.

Nick saw Neel disappear under the table. "If it's not there, try under the bed," Nick said, absently.

What was that glinting on the shelf? Some sort of shiny cylinder?

"Did you find it?"

A muffled response meant Neel was still searching. Reaching up, Nick grasped the cylinder and brought it down. It was rather light. It seemed hollow.

Neel emerged from under the table, crawled over to the bed, and fell to his belly to peer underneath. The bed was much lower than the table. He wriggled his way in.

Turning the cylinder around, Nick noticed a bulb at the other end. It was a flashlight. He'd never seen one like this. It was dented, old. Maybe he could shine it under the bed to help Neel out.

He pressed a little black button he found on the side. Nothing. It probably didn't have any batteries. Or maybe it was spoilt. He unscrewed the end of the cylinder and looked in. Sure enough, no batteries.

There was a muffled shriek from under the bed. Nick hoped Neel had found the ball and not a lizard or rat. He hopped onto the chair just in case. Neel came out from under the bed, butt first. "Found it!" he said, looking around for Nick as he got to his feet. His face was streaked with grey and his clothes were festooned with long strings of dirt and cobwebs like some ghoulish Christmas tree.

"What are you doing up on that chair?" he asked, puzzled.

"Oh. Just getting a view of the room. In case there was something we had overlooked," said Nick, casually dismounting. "Where's the ball?"

Neel held it up, eyes shining in triumph.

"Yes!" Nick pumped his arm. "Okay, quick. Let's go get you changed. You're disgusting."

"What? Not even a thank you?" asked Neel, frowning. "Next time, *you're* going under the bed!"

Neel strode off, and Nick followed sheepishly after.

CHAPTER 3

An Interesting Find

Nick sat cross-legged on the floor watching Neel turn over the flashlight in his hands. The flashlight was golden yet chipped at the edges where specks of rust had begun to appear. The ridges along its length made a simple, decorative pattern and there were minor dents on the sides. The glass protecting the bulb was intact, though the mirror was badly scuffed, with parts rubbed away.

"It looks really old," said Neel. "It must be at least as old as Didu!"

"Yeah, I wonder if it works," said Nick. "It would be cool to bring it back to school to show everyone. It might be a rare antique, might be valuable."

Neel pressed the little button on the side. Nothing happened.

"I already tried it back in the studio," said Nick. "Needs new batteries."

"I know where we can get some," said Neel. "Mesho keeps a flashlight in the drawer next to his bed. We can just use the batteries from those!"

He bounded out of the room, returning in a few moments with Mesho's flashlight, which he set down next to the one Nick was holding. Its plastic molding looked cheap and ugly in comparison to the metallic grandeur of the boys' find.

Nick unscrewed Mesho's flashlight, tilting it onto his palm so the batteries slid out into his hand. He unscrewed the back of the old flashlight and pushed one battery into the chamber.

To his surprise, it went in just halfway and wouldn't go further in. Even a gentle tap didn't help. Nick pulled it out and tried sliding in the other battery. That got stuck too.

"Odd," Nick muttered. "These seem to be the right size and the cylinder is definitely made for two batteries."

"Let me try!" said Neel.

He stood the flashlight on its face, inserted a battery and, before Nick could stop him, gave it a whack with the side of his fist. Something seemed to give way inside and the battery shot in.

"No-!" shouted Nick, stopping himself just in time to avoid waking up the household. "What have you done!" he continued in an angry whisper. "You've broken something, maybe the switch mechanism. Now it won't work at all. Who knows how valuable this might have been. Now it's ruined!"

Neel looked a bit startled. He hadn't actually expected his effort to make any difference. Nick quickly picked up the flashlight and turned it over to inspect the glass. The battery slid back out and dropped to the floor. He paid no attention to it.

"Thank God the glass is okay!" he said, turning his attention now to the inside of the flashlight. He peered in. Nothing seemed to be bent or broken. The button, too, seemed to work just as before.

"Nick," said a small voice at his elbow. "Something fell out."

"Yeah, yeah, I know - the battery," muttered Nick, still peering into the cylinder with one eye, the other one closed. He looked just like a sniper taking aim at a distant target.

"No, there's something else," said Neel, holding up a little yellow object that looked like it came from inside the flashlight. His eyes had gone moist.

Nick put down the flashlight and turned to what Neel was handing him. He took it in his hand. It was a piece of paper, wrapped around something hard.

"This is really weird." said Nick, contemplating the piece, "I'm sure flashlights don't come with bits like this tucked inside them."

"Really?" asked Neel hopefully.

"It looks like a piece of paper. Hang on," said Nick, thrusting the flashlight into Neel's hand. "And please don't drop it. Just hold on to it - don't do anything else!"

"Can I screw the bottom back on?" asked Neel, having recovered his spirits.

"Fine," said Nick, fiddling with the wrapping, "Just be careful!"

Nick found a loose end to the paper and gently tugged at it, unfolding the wrapping like a precious little envelope. Whatever was inside was small. He didn't want it to slip through his fingers.

Neel, who had put the flashlight back together and was clinging tightly to it, was watching Nick unfold the paper. Bit by bit it opened to reveal a small, hard, black object about an inch long. Nick lifted up the paper and the object dropped into his palm.

"What is it?" asked Neel, breathlessly.

"Kind of like a strange key," said Nick, holding it up to the light between his thumb and forefinger. "See? It's got a round hole at the back and a couple of tooth-like things at the end. But the teeth aren't on the same side, like with normal keys. They're on different sides."

Nick examined it further. "And it's hollow, not solid. This may be a key but it's nothing like anything I've seen before."

The boys turned their attention to the paper, which Nick was still holding in his left hand. It was old, as old as the flashlight. It was creased where the folds had been and you could even see light through some of the more frayed parts. It may have been white once, but the paper had gone dark yellow, almost brown towards the edges and the folds.

"Maybe it was wrapping paper," said Neel. "It's got some decoration."

"Seems like an odd design," said Nick, studying it closely. "Wrapping paper should have patterns or maybe flowers or pictures on it. This doesn't have any symmetry."

"Oh wait!" said Neel, "Could it be writing? Maybe someone has written a note?"

"Ah good thinking," said Nick. He held the paper up to the light. At first, all he could make out were loops and curls and flourishes, nothing like any handwriting Nick had seen. Worse, the ink was faded in parts and the folds and tears made it almost impossible to make out anything.

"That looks like 'nobody'," he mused, peering at the center of the paper. "And that one at the end looks like 'door'... and maybe that's 'where'... Neel, you're right. This is a note. But it's going to take some real hard work to figure out what it says. I can't just hold it up to the sun – we'll need much better light. And it'll just fall apart if I keep holding it up like this. Someone - I don't know who - hid this key inside the flashlight and the note probably explains what to do with it."

"Yep!" said Neel, still clutching the flashlight. "Nick, do you - do you think we have a mystery on our hands?"

Nick looked over at Neel, whose little round face was looking eagerly back at him.

"Yes," he said beaming back. "Yes, Nilu. I do think we have a mystery on our hands."

CHAPTER 4

Nick Goes Nuts

The next morning Mashi served breakfast at eight. Mashi always served breakfast at eight. Nick was a picky eater, and mealtimes in Kolkata were a running nightmare. Mashi took special pleasure in making Nick eat everything that he detested, fixing him with a stern gaze till his plate was licked clean.

This morning, breakfast consisted of a yucky runny egg, which Nick detested. He sat stricken, watching toast mash up with sticky yolk and saliva into a warm, gooey mess in Neel's mouth. Round and round it went as Neel, painfully aware of his brother's distress, opened his jaws extra wide to provide Nick an unobstructed view. Something oozed out of the corner of Neel's mouth and dripped onto his plate. Nick almost gagged. His little brother's eyes danced as he took in all of Nick's glorious misery.

When Nick looked over, his aunt was staring at him like a Dementor from Harry Potter. Resistance was futile. He took a swig of milk, then tore off some

bread and gingerly dabbed a corner of it into his egg. He screwed up his eyes and tried to stuff the entire piece into his mouth, chewing rapidly. It was taking too long. He thought he felt a string of gooey egg white against his lip. He couldn't take it anymore. It was all going to come back up.

Nick's eyes flew open. He stood up, knocking his chair back. CRASH it went to the floor, but he was past caring. He screwed up his face as he rushed to get water. His hands shook as he unscrewed the bottle cap and took a big gulp, shut his eyes again and chomped away at what was left of the bread.

By the time Nick had realized what he'd done the whole family were dead still and staring back at him. His chair lay on the floor. It had narrowly missed the glass vessels full of tea, sugar and salt on the shelves behind him. There was even a puddle of water at his feet, all over the kitchen floor.

Mashi's face was red, redder than from the heat of the oven. Nick had never seen her look so angry. She looked like she would have a stroke. Needless to say, it didn't end well.

Ten minutes later he had been grounded to Didu's room and Neel, accessory to the crime, had been made to follow. After reading Nick the riot act, Ma had stormed out of the room.

"Why can't you just eat your food like a normal person? It's just egg, it's not poison!" said Neel, rehashing the highlights of Ma's speech.

"Enough!" Nick snapped back. "I've heard enough from Ma. The last thing I want is a lesson from you too."

"We could have been solving the mystery by now," Neel went on. "I found the clue and I ate my egg. Why am I being punished?"

"Look," said Nick, "I'm really sorry for causing all the trouble. But there's nothing we can do about it now. Let's just get through the day. We'll be back to solving the mystery tomorrow, okay? I'll even play cricket with you whenever you want."

"What's the point? You'll just end up doing the same things and we'll be back in trouble."

"No. I won't. I promise. In fact, I won't even bat. You can do the batting and I'll just bowl. Is that fair?"

"Promise?"

"Promise."

"And you'll bowl for as long as I want?" asked Neel, brightening up.

Nick sighed. "I'll bowl you... I'll bowl you ten overs." He wondered whether he had over-promised. With Neel you never knew when he'd turn the situation to his advantage.

"A hundred overs," went Neel.

"No. Not a hundred overs. A hundred overs will take the entire day. It makes no sense. I'll do fifteen overs. Fifteen and that's it. That's ninety balls, two hours. And remember I have to do all the fielding as well. Fifteen overs is a lot."

"Okay," chirped Neel. He'd honestly not expected to get more than maybe six.

Later that morning, Nick was expected to help Mesho with the shopping as punishment. Neel, thoroughly enjoying his brother's peril, had eagerly tagged along. He had even forgotten about the note and the flashlight, for now.

Nick was hoping that the trip to the market wouldn't take too long. That was before he saw the armfuls of shopping bags Mesho was carrying. His heart sank. Mesho had a large jute bag and loads of plastic bags of varying shapes and sizes stuffed within each other, which was never a good sign.

Before they left, Mesho stopped to tuck the various little bags into the jute bag. Reaching into his pocket, he fished out a piece of paper. Nick recognized Mashi's handwriting. It was a list of all the things they would need to pick up. He spotted tomatoes on it, onions and potatoes. Cauliflower, brinjal and bitter gourd. Even beetroot. Just the thought of beetroot made Nick gag again.

All afternoon the sun bored down and it did nothing for Nick's mood as they haggled their way through the market. Mesho was a gold medalist at bargain-hunting, a skill he kept sharp. He didn't let even a lemon go a-begging without getting a discount.

"But sir, the lemon is only three rupees. How can I give you a rupee off?" pleaded one vegetable-monger.

"I come to you first every time. Every time," lied Mesho. "How long have I been coming to you first? Should I start going to the others instead?"

"No, no, sir, how can I allow that? You are my most loyal customer!" replied the vendor, who had just observed Mesho patronize two other vegetable stalls before him. "You take the discount, no problem. I will give you one rupee off like you ask."

He started packing the bag Mesho proffered him.

"... and some chilies," said Mesho pressing the advantage.

"... and some chilies," nodded the man dutifully tossing in a handful.

This was all made ten times worse by Neel. To keep him engaged, Mesho had given him the task of ticking items off the list. But it seemed like Neel was actually enjoying it. In fact, he had even made them retrace their steps when he realized they'd missed getting a sprig of coriander. For his diligence, Mesho had given Neel a chocolate éclair and a pat on his head. Nick had wanted to smack him.

On the way home, and as they were passing the sweetshop, Nick noticed that the little photocopy shop at the end of the street was unusually busy.

"Mesho why are there so many people lined up there?" he asked.

"Oh them?" said Mesho. "College students. Their exams are round the corner so they're probably getting notes copied. Some of them even get entire books copied here to save money on buying them new. But between you and me, he's a bit of a crook."

Neel's ears pricked up at this. "Why do you call him a crook?"

"Sometimes I think he makes the copies come out wrong so he can charge twice for the same job. He did that to me once, so now I don't go to him anymore" said Mesho.

"How does he make them come out wrong?" asked Nick.

"Um. He makes it darker or lighter. The copies. You can set the machine to do that. Then if you can't read it, he has to do it again."

Nick nodded.

After they got back Nick was herded into Didu's room for the rest of the day. No books, no iPad, just his thoughts for company. Nick kept thinking about the torch and the note. He had really wanted to work it all out today. He'd been thinking about them all afternoon at the market.

When they were called down for dinner that evening, the steel serving pots were neatly laid out on the center of the table with lids on. Plates and spoons were set on tablemats, and Didu, Mashi, Mesho and Ma had already taken their places. Baba was meeting a professor at Presidency College and would be late returning home.

Nick pulled up a chair and sat down. Neel trotted up a few moments later and took his place beside him.

Mashi removed the lids as Nick braced himself for the culinary torture that would surely follow.

"What's this?" he asked, gaping at the spread before him. Where was the pukey pumpkin, the ghastly gourd and beastly brinjal? There wasn't even any yucky yam or rotten radish. Instead there were lentils and cauliflower and fish - and a bowl of sweets at every plate.

Was this the right house, wondered Nick, looking around at the family. Did he take the wrong turn and blunder into a neighbor's doorway by mistake?

'Slurp' went Neel, stuffing his mouth with rice and lentils. "Shom cawifower pleesh?"

Mashi served him a ladleful. "Would you like some?" she asked Nick in her trademark monotone. The corners of her mouth seemed to be twitching.

"Yes please, Mashi."

Was he imagining it? Could that be a smile, Nick wondered as he held out his plate. Nah!

The rest of the meal passed pleasantly enough. Nick ate in silence as the family chatted away. He still couldn't digest this strange turn of events. Neel took three helpings of everything.

"Are you going to finish that?" he asked Nick, pointing to a few pieces of potato Nick had left on the side of his plate. "Guess not!" he said, reaching out to spoon them over to his plate.

Nick took his plate to the washbasin and rinsed it off. The helper would wash the utensils next morning. The boys went upstairs to wash up and get ready for bed.

The day was done and so, it seemed, was their punishment.

CHAPTER 5

A Fruitless Morning

Neel woke up to the hazy outlines of Nick sitting up next to him, studying something. He rubbed his eyes and looked at the little alarm clock next to the pillow. It was 7 am. Pretty early for Nick to be up reading.

He nudged Nick with his elbow. Nick waved the note at him briefly before getting back to it.

The riddle! Neel was instantly awake.

"Well?" he asked Nick.

"I think it's going to be very hard," Nick said, looking dolefully at the note. "I'm hardly able to make out anything. All we have so far are three words, which make no sense together - 'nobody', 'where' and 'door'! We need to shine a light through the paper to be able to read more and the light in this room is just not working."

Neel sighed. This was turning into a real drag. He wished Nick could just figure out the clue so they could start exploring already. He felt certain there was something exciting just waiting to be discovered.

"Nick," he said. "We've tried it your way. It's not working. Why don't we just take the key and try it on all the doors? Maybe we'll get lucky. Maybe we'll find the lock without the clue?"

Nick nodded doubtfully. It was worth a try. In any case he had run out of ideas. Perhaps a break would do him good. He could come back to the note with a fresh mind. He folded the note and slipped it into his pocket.

"Okay, let's do it," said Nick. "Should we start by making a list of all the rooms so we can knock them off one by one?"

"Yeah," said Neel.

Nick headed towards the writing desk.

"Or," started Neel, "we could just go round all the rooms one by one. How about that?"

Nick turned to him. He thought for a moment. "Alright then. Let's start with the rooms on the ground floor and work up," said Nick making his way to the door.

"Don't forget the key!" said Neel sliding it out of the flashlight and clasping it firmly in his hand. He rushed out behind Nick.

The two of them made their way quietly down the stairs to the courtyard. Neel had to do his best to control his urge to rush ahead. The thumping of his slippers would have definitely woken up someone and brought their adventure to a premature end.

"Let's start on the left and work our way around," said Nick. "Then we can make our way further up. That way we won't miss anything."

Neel nodded. They made their way to the first door on the left. It was a narrow door that the boys had never seen opened, a very promising start.

Neel darted forward and held up the lock in his hand. It was rather small. His excitement mounted. He tried the key but it didn't fit. He jiggled and angled it to make one of the teeth go in, but it was no use. The key simply did not fit.

"It's no use," said Nick as Neel made one more attempt to get the key in. "That lock's new and shiny. It's just like all the other locks you see all over the place. It's small but it isn't the right one for this old key."

Neel stepped back reluctantly. This was a promising door though. Too bad the lock wasn't the right one.

The next one in line was the bathroom. Being old, it did not have running water and was instead supplied with ice-cold groundwater drawn through a bore well. Neel hated taking a bath in there. Each mug of water would make him jump out of his skin!

"Brrr," went Neel. "We already know there's nothing there," he said, pressing on to the next door.

Nick stayed where he was. "Hold on. We don't know for sure. Just because a room is used doesn't mean it's not the right one. Let's just try it. We're here already, what's the harm?"

"Well, there's no lock on the door," said Neel holding up the bare latch and shaking it.

"But there might be a keyhole in the door itself. Did you check for that?" asked Nick, coming closer and bending down to bring his eye to the level of the latch.

There was none, so they moved to the next door.

The next two doors they tried had locks but they were relatively new and the key wouldn't fit them. Neither was a surprise, since they were well used - one for receiving visitors and the other a storeroom that had once been Mesho's studio.

Ground floor done, they moved up to the first floor and tried their luck room by room, taking care not to make too much noise. Luckily, the little sound they did make was drowned out by the early morning whistles and clangs from the kitchen.

It had been about half an hour. Their efforts so far had yielded nothing but disappointment. They had tried all the doors in the house, working their way up to the terrace. In an inspired moment, they had even gone back to check the mailbox and the door of the enclosure protecting the electric bore well pump. None of them were the right ones.

They stood in front of the last door, the attic room. One more time they peeked at the jumbled furniture

inside, like they had done across so many summers. But this time was very different.

"Last one," said Neel, looking up at Nick. His face was flushed and his eyes a little moist. Unlike the others, this lock was old and bulky, a black blob that felt heavy. The keyhole was covered with a little metal flap. It looked like it was built to secure important things.

This is it, thought Neel as he lifted the flap out of the way and brought the key up to the lock. His hands shook with excitement. What secrets would the room reveal?

The key went in easily but, when he tried to turn it, it just wiggled. He forced it a little, putting both hands on the key.

"Sorry, Neel," Nick said from behind. "This isn't the right one either. If it were, the key would have turned much easier than this. I think the key is too small for this lock. It's not the right door…"

Neel's shoulders slumped and he let go of the key, which remained hanging from the keyhole. He looked back at Nick, crestfallen. He had been so sure.

"Can *you* try, Nick?" he asked. A little tear formed on the corner of his eye.

Nick studied the face of his sad little brother. "Sure," he said.

He gave it a couple of tries, various angles, but it was a lost cause.

"It's okay, Nilu," he said. "We still have the note. We'll figure it out. I'm sure of it."

Neel nodded slowly. This was no adventure. Dejected, he followed Nick down the stairs and back to Didu's room.

Neel slumped to the floor. He was a picture of misery. Nick, too.

Neel wanted nothing more to do with this entire thing. Why would someone leave a key that didn't fit anything? He flung the key down on the bed. He was done. Nick could pursue it by himself or throw it away for all he cared. This had promised to be the best summer of his life. Instead it had gone back to being long, hot and boring. Just like every summer. Oh, why did God have to show him this mirage, only to whisk it away? He slumped to the floor and closed his eyes.

Nick sat on a chair, pinching his lower lip. They had to figure out that note. The note had the answer. He could feel it in his bones.

CHAPTER 6

Deciphering the Clue

It was afternoon and the house was still. Nick was still poring over the note. Neel, on the other hand, was rolling around on the cool floor and going through his reading assignment from school. The book took his mind off things, put him in a better mood.

A few minutes passed before Nick looked up once again. He smiled at the sight of Neel rolling around.

"If we ever get bored of cricket, at least we know where to get a soccer ball," said Nick playfully. Neel seemed to be back to his usual cheerful self. Maybe he could even entice him back to mystery-solving.

Neel continued what he was doing.

"I'm not having much success with this note, to be honest," Nick said loudly to himself. "Maybe I should try shining the flashlight through the paper."

Neel looked at him out of the corner of his eye.

Nick spotted Neel's glance but pretended he didn't notice. He fetched Mesho's flashlight from the drawer. It might have looked ugly but it would definitely do a better job than the vintage piece.

He held up the note in his left hand and the flashlight in his right, shining the light through the paper. It was a definite improvement. Weaker scribbles sharpened into sight, but he couldn't read them. The paper was fluttering too much.

"Here Neel," he called out. "Could you please hold the flashlight?"

Neel turned his back to Nick. He couldn't be bothered to get up from this comfortable position for another wild goose chase. Let Nick figure it out if he wants.

Shifting his position, Nick placed the flashlight between his knees and got a good hold of the paper.

"J... e... w... is that another e maybe? And then I think there's an 's'," said Nick bringing the paper right up to his nose. "Jew... s."

Neel stopped moving.

"Jews?" mused Nick, pinching his lip. "Were there Jews in Kolkata? But why's there a gap in the word?"

"Jew—s... Jew—s... Oh!" said Nick, sitting up a few inches. "It's - it's jewels. The word is jewels. Neel!"

Neel let out a little squeak. In a flash, he leapt up onto the bed next to Nick. Nick pointed to the word. It did indeed look like 'jewels', Neel decided.

"Here, give *me* the flashlight," said Neel, snatching it away from Nick. He kept it steady while

Nick held up the note in front of it, squinting at the paper and moving it back and forth to try and make out the words. Was that a 'y' or a 'j'? And was that other bit even a word or just a smudge?

"That's it," he said. "That's all I can make out, even with the flashlight. The ink is just too faint. Whoever wrote this note expected it to be found earlier."

Wait. Wasn't there some way to make things darker?

He racked his brain. Darker… darker... who was talking about it the other day?

Neel was back to making moaning noises about the injustice of life but he tuned him out.

Think, Nick, *think*!

And then he had it! The photocopy crook!

"Neel, come with me," he ordered, cutting into Neel's running diatribe about life. "Put on your shoes and bring me my wallet. I think I have the answer."

Nick prodded Ma, who was gently snoring on the bed next to them.

"Ma… Ma… hey Ma! Are you listening?"

Ma's eyelids fluttered. "Wha-?"

"Ma, we're just going to the photocopy shop," whispered Nick.

"Wha-? Why?" Ma asked, half-rising from the bed. "Did Baba ask you for something?"

"No," replied Nick, heading to the door. "Just wanted to show Neel how it works." He knew Ma would never question anything that involved learning, especially if it meant keeping Neel out of trouble for any length of time.

"Oh, okay then. Come back soon!"

Ma lay back down. A little smile played on her lips. As the summer holidays wore on, the boys typically got onto each other's' nerves. By now they should have been pulling each other's' hair out. Instead, for the past few days, they'd been joined at the hip. Thank heaven for small mercies!

"Are you done yet?" called Nick from the front door as Neel struggled with his shoes.

"Coming, coming," he yelled hopping on one foot while trying to put a shoe on the other, afraid Nick would get fed up and just leave him behind. "Just give me one sec!"

He stumbled onto the street with one heel out. "Ready!" he said, stamping his foot to try and get it in.

"Hold on," said Nick, kneeling down, untying Neel's laces and sliding his foot in. Another minute or two wouldn't change anything.

Shoes in place, the boys started off. The photocopy shop was right around the corner from home.

"Did you bring the note?" panted Neel, half-running to keep up with Nick's long strides.

Nick patted his shirt pocket.

They soon reached the photocopy shop. Nick got there first, with a wheezing Neel trailing a few meters behind. 'XEROX PCO LOCAL STD ISD' proclaimed the board outside.

"Mister!" called Nick through the doorway. "Mister, we need help copying something!"

Neel panted up to Nick. "This - was - a - lot - further - than - you - said," he said, bending over and holding the doorframe for support.

"Mister! Hey Mister, where are you?" called Nick once again.

"Hold your horses, young man," said an annoyed-sounding voice from behind them, "Your books aren't running away and neither will my machine. Just wait a few minutes."

He squeezed past them and sat down on a stool next to his photocopier, peering at Nick over his glasses. "Look here, what did you want copied? If it's more than a few pages you'll have to come back later. I have a pile of other jobs to do first."

"Hi Mister! I needed this one page copied, but the writing on it is very faint. Someone told me you could adjust your machine to make writing come out clearer. Can you help us? Please?"

"What do you have?" he asked.

"Just this old note," said Nick, suddenly realizing he should have thought of a better story. Behind him, Neel rolled his eyes. Nick really needed some lessons in storytelling.

"Show me," said the man, holding out his hand.

Nick placed the piece of paper gingerly into the man's open palm. Pushing his glasses firmly onto his nose, the man peered near-sightedly at it.

"This ink is completely faded," he said, after examining it for a while. "It might not come out properly at all - and even if it does, the dark parts of the paper will come out darker and hide it. The whole thing might be a waste!"

"It's okay, Mister. We have to try," said Nick. "It's important."

No sooner had he said the last words did Nick realize he should not have mentioned its importance. The man suddenly perked up.

"Important, you say? Why?" asked the man, stroking his chin. Perhaps he could charge the kids extra for this job.

"Oh, nothing special. It's not *important* important. Just kind of important," said Nick, trying desperately to cover up. Behind him, Neel was fidgeting with his fingers. What on earth was Nick doing?

"Well, which is it?" asked the man, irritably. "Is it important or is it not? I have piles of work to do and here you are barging in and speaking in riddles. Go somewhere else and don't waste my time!"

With that, the man got up, turned his back on them and started shuffling some paper around. Unless the boys could think of something the conversation was over.

"Please Sir," piped up Neel. "Please help us. This note is by our great-grandfather. We only have this to remember him. Me and my brother wanted to take a photocopy to frame, for our mum's birthday."

The man paused in his work for a second.

"... but we understand if you have other things to do. Thank you for your time," said Neel dolefully. "Come, Nick, let's go. We can buy Ma a card instead." He started shuffling towards the door.

"Okay, okay, come back!" said the man. "Why couldn't you just explain earlier instead of talking in circles and confusing me? I can try it but it'll cost you five rupees a copy."

"Five?" began Nick. "But it normally costs just-"

"It's okay, Mister. Five will be fine," said Neel, kicking Nick on the shin. "You'll do it now? Please? We have to get back soon."

The man walked over to his machine and placed the paper face down on the glass plate and gently closed the lid. He thought for some time. Then he punched a few buttons. Nick crept up closer to see what he was doing.

"Back, back," said the man, waving Nick away. "Please stay away from the machine. It's very expensive." Nick retreated a few steps and craned his neck to see what the man was doing.

Adjustments done, the man thumbed a large, well-worn green button. The machine clattered to life. It made a few tentative noises and then a bright light flashed under the lid. With a soothing hum, it slid from one end to the other, darting back to the starting point once it had reached the other end.

Fwip. A piece of paper flew out onto the tray. Nick grabbed at it with both hands and turned it over to see the results. It was useless. Everything was dark and blotchy. Except for a couple of words on the corner, he couldn't make out anything at all. Even the words they had figured out earlier had dissolved into the stains.

"Mister," he moaned. "It didn't work..."

The man took the sheet from Nick and examined it calmly. "Look, son, this kind of thing is exactly what I expected. But I think I can do better than this. It will take a few tries to get the settings right. But it will cost you five rupees per copy. Are you okay to pay?"

"How many tries?" asked Nick.

"Oh, I don't know. Maybe five or six?"

Thirty rupees! Nick rummaged in his wallet. Including coins, he had just about eighteen rupees, enough for three tries. And one was already done!

"I only have enough for three. Please try to make it work in three attempts."

"I can definitely try," said the man. "No promises though."

He got to work again, adjusting some settings up, others down. Even he was kind of excited by the challenge.

While they waited, Nick and Neel studied the spoilt copy. It was hard to make out anything. However, they did notice that the top left corner was now in sharp focus. They could now make out a couple of new words.

"'I've hidden'," read out Neel.

"Yeah," said Nick, "And there's another word after it. The one after that was the word 'where'. So the first line reads 'I've hidden something where'. And then we had the other words - nobody and treasure."

Fwip. Out came another copy. The man picked it up and had a look.

"This one is okay?" he asked, handing the paper over to Nick.

This version was a lighter than the previous one, but darker than the original. Nick was able to spot a new set of words on this one - 'care' on the second line and then 'Behind' something.

"No, no Mister, sorry," said Nick, "It's not done yet. Can you please make sure it is perfect this time? We have only one more chance."

"Look children, the way the note is faded and discolored, I'm sorry but there is no way to make it come out perfectly. I could make another try but remember you have to pay for each copy. You already owe me ten rupees."

"It's okay Mister. We can pay for one more. We're sure you can do it," said Nick. They were so close now.

"Don't say I didn't warn you," said the man, once again making adjustments to the machine.

Neel pushed his way forward and pressed right up next to the machine, watching the changes the man was making.

"C'mon, c'mon," Neel muttered from between clenched teeth.

Nick put the two sheets next to each other and gazed at them, trying hard to calm his racing heartbeat. Looking around, he noticed a red ballpoint pen on the desk. He could use it to mark out what they had so far. It would keep his mind off that dratted third copy.

Removing the cover, he started marking out words on the sheets.

I've hidden ______ where

The adjustments were done. The man looked up at Neel and gave him a thumbs-up sign.

Nobody ______ care

"Ready?" he asked.

______ *jewels* ______ ______ (Nick couldn't help smiling at this one)

"... ready," said Neel, after a moment's pause. It was now or never!

Behind Nan_____ _______

"Wait!" called out Nick, just as the man was about to press the button. He caught himself just in time, head jerking towards Nick. Neel, too, turned to look at him.

"Wait Mister, just give me one second. I think I know what you need to do."

"Huh? You do, do you?" scoffed the man. "I'll have you know I've done this for years, decades even. And you think you can tell me how to do my work? Why, I've been here since-"

"Mister, do you have a blue pen?" asked Nick, completely ignoring his outburst. Receiving no answer, Nick looked around and spotted one in the man's pocket.

"Neel, could you pass the pen?" asked Nick, indicating the pen in the man's pocket.

Still looking a bit unsettled, Neel slipped the pen out and brought it over to Nick, who underlined the gap words on the second copy.

"Look, Mister, we don't actually need a perfect copy. Can you just fix these parts I've underlined here? We can piece together what was written between the three copies. And then we can just frame the original and write up the message as part of the gift."

Nick handed the underlined copy back to the man, who stopped gaping at Nick and took a look at the paper.

"You kids and your silly riddles," said the man. "Let me see what I can do."

He went back to his machine. A few seconds later, *fwip,* it came out and the man picked it up. He studied it carefully and grinned. He tossed the paper light-heartedly at Nick who quickly scanned it. By Jove, he'd done it!

"Sir, you are the king of photocopy people! When I grow up I'll get my textbooks photocopied at your shop. So will Neel!" cheered Nick, doing a little jig and shaking Neel till his teeth rattled in his head.

"Enough, enough. That'll be fifteen rupees!" said the man, officiously. He liked the kids, but his very expensive machine was placed precariously on a stool and there was no need to encourage all this tomfoolery in his cramped little shop.

Nick emptied out his wallet and gave him everything while Neel collected the note as well as its three copies.

"Here you go, sir, eighteen rupees for your trouble. Thanks a lot!"

The man waved goodbye to the boys as they ran back up the street.

"Bye, bye, Mister! Remember to change back your settings!" yelled Neel from the corner. "You don't want everyone to get bad copies, do you?"

At that, the old man's expression changed. His eyes widened as he stared at them running off in the distance. What did that boy mean?

***

Back at the house, Nick sat at the writing desk with the copies spread out in front of him while Neel sat on the edge of the desk. Picking up his notepad and pen, Nick wrote out the entire message.

He leaned back on his chair and sighed. Finally, some progress.

“I wonder who Nanima is? Or was. And why did this writer just sign her name as Mrs.? Mrs. what? And what are these treasures?” asked Nick, to nobody in particular.

Beside him, Neel was beaming. Life had suddenly gotten a lot more interesting.

They were on a real-life treasure hunt.

CHAPTER 7

Family History

"Ma," asked Nick, trying to look innocent as they settled down to have lunch. "Ma, this house has so many rooms. There must have been loads of people living here. Tell us about more of your family. Please?"

Nick and Neel had agreed that the most direct course of action was to figure out who Nanima was and find her room. That would lead them to the treasure.

"Umm," said Ma, flattered that Nick wanted to know more about her family. "Well there's your other uncle and aunt, of course, the ones who currently live in Bhopal. Then there's Didu - and Dadu before he died. Dadu had three brothers, your granduncles. And then there was my grandfather and grandmother. They were the ones to build this house, when your grandpa and his brothers were just children. That's all I think."

"Weren't the brothers married?" asked Nick, taking mental notes. This was going to be a long list of people. He hoped he could remember everything.

"Yeah, of course, two of them were," said Ma between mouthfuls of food. "One had twin children, who also married twins, can you imagine? The other had a boy and a girl. All of them are my cousins, hence your more distant uncles and aunts. They live in different places in India - Jaipur, Ranchi..."

"Oh, so what were their names?"

"Wow, so many questions today! What happened?" asked Anna, interjecting herself into the conversation. "Don't you even know the names of your own uncles and aunts?"

She began counting off names on her clean left hand as she picked at her fish and rice with her right. "There's Asit, the eldest, then Arati. Neither of them is married. Then we have the twins Anju and Manju, who married Rabi and Kabi, and finally Salil, who married Bonu. There you have it - eight uncles and aunts. That's right, isn't it mom?"

She looked at Mashi for approval and Mashi beamed back. Ma looked on approvingly.

"You're absolutely right," exclaimed Ma in wonder. "Nick, why can't you be more like Anna?"

"Well, I'm trying," he mumbled into his food. "If nobody tells me anything how would I know?"

Ma settled back to her meal. Nick made a mental note of all the names - none of them sounded like Nanima.

"Well smarty-pants, if you know so much, what are the names of Dadu's brothers and sisters-in-law?" asked Neel, trying to help Nick along.

"Glad you asked," said Anna, sitting up in her most school-principal-like fashion. "The eldest was Sailendra, who married Jyotsna. Then there were Jatindra and Phanindra, neither of whom ever married. And of course, we have our very own Dadu and Didu - Sudhindra and Rama."

Neel rolled his eyes. This was just too much. Nick, despite himself, was impressed.

"And what was great-grandfather's name?" asked Mashi, proud of her daughter.

"Manas Ranjan Sen - and *his* wife was called Sushobha! I think that's the entire family tree."

"You sure?" asked Nick. "Didn't leave out any twigs or leaves by any chance?"

"Quite sure," said Anna, missing the sarcasm in Nick's question.

Nick had to try something, fast, before this opportunity slipped by. It would be weird to bring up the subject in future, especially as he'd shown zero interest in his ancestors in the past. Ma would be sure to start asking uncomfortable questions.

"Well then," he thundered, in the manner of a TV lawyer about to unmask the perpetrator. "Why did you leave out - Nanima?"

There was sudden silence. Anna stared at Nick like he'd gone mad.

"Who on Earth is Nanima?" asked Anna. She looked shocked. Was there something she didn't know that Nick did?

"Mom, who's Nanima?" she asked her mother, plaintively. But Mashi, too, was looking puzzled.

"I have no idea..."

Ma, too, seemed to have no clue about what Nick was saying. Nick grew a little hot around his ears.

"Nanima. There was definitely a Nanima," he said bravely to the incredulous group at the table.

"I don't know," said Ma. "Oh wait, here's Didu. She might know who you're talking about."

"What's all this?" asked Didu, shuffling through the kitchen door and lowering herself painfully down the one step from the threshold to the floor. Of late her knees had really been giving her trouble, so that she had to start shifting her weight from side to side when she walked, looking for all the world like a kindly little penguin. Despite her pain, the kids had never seen her anything but cheerful. Soft, smiling, full of stories and ready for a game of Ludo any evening, she was exactly what anyone could want in a granny.

"Did I hear someone call my name? Who has time for a little old lady like me?" She said, sitting down at the table with a little sigh.

"Didu, Didu..." went Anna before the boys could say anything, "Nick claims there was someone called Nanima in our family, but nobody seems to know anything about this person. Tell him it's not true. I'm sure he's just making it up to make me look bad!"

Nick looked at Didu with bated breath. Was she going to shatter their dreams? Didu merely smiled. For a second, her eyes took on a faraway look. She turned to Nick.

"Where did you hear about Nanima?" she asked.

"So it's true?" yelped Nick, partly in excitement and partly to deflect a question he'd rather not answer.

"Nanima was the name given to my mother-in-law, your Dadu's mother," Didu said, in a voice that had suddenly thickened with memories.

"But Didu, her name was Sushobha!" piped up Anna, with a mixture of surprise and chagrin. How had Nick outsmarted her?

"Shush!" said Mashi, eager to learn more about this mystery moniker. Was there actually something about her own grandmother she didn't know?

"Yes," said Didu. "Her real name was Sushobha, but my father-in-law would call her Nanima out of affection. He'd whisper it to her when he thought nobody could hear him. But I did. He never found out!" Didu chuckled a bit at the memory.

"Shame, shame, Didu," said Neel. "Why were you spying on them?"

"No silly," retorted Didu. "I'd be flitting about the house doing chores when I'd come across them. It wasn't on purpose, and I always announced myself when I realized I'd intruded on them. But I couldn't very well stop my ears, could I?"

"She was really a great beauty of her time," the old lady continued, as the family listened to her with rapt attention. "Tall - or at least tall for her time - and slim. She had these big eyes that mesmerized anyone who saw her. And she was really modern. She could

play the piano, read and write English. She knew seven Indian languages besides. And my father-in-law doted on her. She was fond of fine clothes and jewelry and he bought her heaps and heaps of them. Every time he went on a business trip, he'd come back with trunks full of silks and pashminas and baubles. This one time, he returned with an amazing pair of earrings shaped like little golden peacocks with feathers made of blue and green stones. But mind you, she had a temper! If anyone crossed her, she would never let them hear the end of it! Even the British soldiers were afraid of her. Especially after one episode when a couple of them had been bothering her from the street below and she threw chili powder right into their faces. They never came near the house again!"

"What a story, Didu," said Anna, dreamily.

Anna was probably imagining herself as the accomplished beauty, thought Nick. Yeah, that'd be the day.

"But where are the jewels and everything?" asked Neel, cutting to the chase. All this was fine, but if there were jewels around, he wanted to have a look at them.

"All gone," sighed Didu.

"Gone?" shot back five voices, almost in unison.

"Gone where?" asked Ma. She would definitely have liked to try on the peacock earrings. It would have made a sensation at the next wedding she attended.

"Stolen, or just sold off," replied Didu. "During Independence, a lot of mansions were looted, and I'm sure they were lost back then. I definitely don't remember Nanima wearing those things in her final years, which would have been quite unimaginable if they were still with her."

"Anyway," she said, suddenly coming back to earth, "You wanted to know who Nanima was, and I've told you. Now let's come back to the present, shall we? What's for lunch?"

Nick shot a glance at Neel, who beamed back at him. Talk about killing two birds with one stone. Not only had they found the answer they needed, they'd also managed to put one over Anna. Not bad, not bad at all!

There was just one more piece of information they needed to solve the mystery.

"Ma," asked Nick that evening as she came to kiss the boys goodnight. "If this room was always Didu's room, where did Nanima sleep?"

"There you go again, with Nanima. Wonder what's gotten into you?"

"So… the room was…?" prompted Nick, worried she'd walk off without completing the thought.

"It was the room next door," she said, pointing at the wall.

Nick thought she was joking. "Ma, be serious! Room next door? Hello, you're pointing to a wall! There's no door there!"

"No, my boy, there *is* a room on the other side. You could walk right through the corridor but the way was walled up when the rooms on the other side were given out on rent. Don't you know we still have tenants in that wing of the house?"

Tenants?

Oh my God, he had totally forgotten about them. That means there were at least five or six rooms they hadn't explored at all. Perhaps the key would fit one of them. Most likely the one right next door, like Ma had said.

They needed a way to search the tenants' rooms, thought Nick. What would they find?

Before he could imagine anything further, Nick had dozed off. Neel lay beside him, curled up with his side pillow, snoring gently. The boys were fast asleep.

CHAPTER 8

The Elusive Door

"Why can't we just go over and meet them?" asked Neel, for maybe the tenth time the next morning.

"We can't just march over to their place and ask to inspect their rooms."

"Why not, they're our tenants?"

"Landlords don't normally send little children over to conduct spot checks. They'd call Mesho the moment we open our mouths. You want that? No. We need a better excuse."

"Excuse for what?" demanded Anna, walking in on them and making Neel jump.

"Sheesh, Anna, can't you knock or something?" grumbled Nick.

"It's *my* house. I can do anything I want. I don't need your permission to enter. Besides I was coming over to get my pen. What were you two whispering about? Don't think I haven't noticed the two of you plotting and sneaking about these past few days.

And then you come up with that weird piece of family trivia? It's too much to be a coincidence."

"Spill it," she said, turning on Nick, "Or I'm going to tell your mum that you're up to no good and she'll make you."

Nick looked at her. Drat that Anna. Wasn't she supposed to be studying? How had she noticed what they were doing?

"Look, it's nothing," he began. "Just some harmless story. That's all. It's childish, really. Nothing you'd be interested in."

"Try me," said Anna, folding her arms and thrusting her hip out. "I have plenty of time right now. I've finished next term's syllabus already."

Nick sighed and glanced at Neel, who had on a pained expression like he'd eaten something bad. He was mortified. Telling Anna was like signing a death warrant on the mystery. She'd shut everything down in an instant and have them locked into the room permanently, for good measure. In fact, *they'd* probably end up being the ones writing notes to help future generations find their bones.

There was nothing for it. She had them in a corner. They were going to have to tell her everything. He signed at her to sit down beside them. It would take a while to cover everything.

"Well..." he began.

Over the next fifteen minutes or so he told her everything. Neel chipped in with details. Anna heard

them out with growing disbelief. Her eyes kept darting from one to the other as they recounted their story.

"So that's how you knew about Nanima," she exclaimed as Nick's narrative came to an end. "I knew there was no way for you to have known something about the family that I didn't."

"Yeah," said Nick.

He hunched over and studied the floor between his crossed legs. It had indeed been an incredible adventure, while it lasted. Reaching over to Neel, he gently patted him on the back. Neel had been an amazing partner in this entire mission - the best he could have asked for. He felt sorrier for Neel than for himself.

"... and Nilu, you were so brave and quick-witted," Anna was saying. "I never imagined the two of you were so clever. I would never have thought of the photocopy idea either - it was just brilliant."

Wait. What?

Anna was *praising* them?

Nick looked up and scanned Anna's face. Her eyes were shining. She looked excited.

"So… we're not in trouble?" he asked, tentatively.

"Trouble? No, silly. Why would you be in trouble? This is such an adventure. That too in *my* house. I want to help. What can I do?"

"Well," Neel jumped in before Nick could say anything. "There is the matter of exploring the tenant's wing. We can't figure out how to get into Nanima's room. Do you have any ideas?"

"Hmmm..." said Anna, looking down and beginning to twirl a lock of her hair. "I do know them a bit. We invite them over to have tea and sweets every Durga Puja…" she continued her musings.

"Hey," Neel cut in. "Then we can just have you go over and get us in!"

"No Neel," said Anna. Nick shook his head too. "Even if I know them, we can't just barge into their house and start ransacking it. We need an excuse. But what?"

She twirled her hair again. Nick began doodling on a blank paper of his notebook. Neel went back to rolling around on the floor and imagining what the treasure would look like. He had exhausted all the options he could think of. He was more a man of action.

"I've got it," said Anna, "Why don't we drop something into their place so we can go over to ask for it back?"

"Nick," she continued, "didn't you guys whack a ball off the terrace once already? Maybe you could 'accidentally' knock it into their part of the house this time?"

Nick could barely believe what he was hearing. Not only was she not snitching on them, she was actually suggesting they get up to some mischief! He reached out and gave Anna's arm a pinch.

"Ouch!" she shrieked, recoiling in pain and surprise. "What did you do that for?"

"I just wanted to make sure I wasn't dreaming and it really was you," said Nick. "Anna asking us to actually do something wrong."

"Nut," she said rubbing her arm. "No this is not a dream. I am trying to help you. And-"

Quick as a flash, Anna jabbed her arm out. She gave Nick's arm a tight pinch, twisting the skin for good effect.

"Yeow!" went Nick.

"... and you check to see whether you're dreaming by pinching yourself, not others. Don't you have any common sense?" finished Anna, sitting back on her hands to admire her handwork. Neel paused his rolling and watched the scene with fascination. This was fun.

"Uff," went Nick, rubbing the pinched area. It was really smarting. He could see nail marks.

"Okay, truce," he gasped once the pain had subsided somewhat. "So we just throw the ball into their side of the house?"

"Yeah, something like that. Then we can go over to ask for the ball."

"But why would they let us into the rooms? Wouldn't they just tell us to get the ball and leave?"

"Yeah, I thought of that," said Anna. She turned to look at Neel. "When we go in, Neel needs to fake a bathroom visit - a big job, not the little one - to buy us some time."

"Wait, what do you mean big job?" asked Neel, suspiciously.

"You know, Big Job," said Anna looking meaningfully at him.

A grin spread across Nick's face. "Yeah, Neel, you have a Big Job to do," he said, starting to laugh now.

Neel's expression changed. He stood and drew himself up to his full height. "Nick, Anna. Do you think I'm four years old? I don't just go the toilet any old time. I'm a big boy."

"That's why we need you to do the Big Job," went Nick, tears starting to form around his eyes.

"Stop it, Nick," whined Neel. "It's not funny!"

"Sorry, sorry," said Nick, burying his face in a pillow.

"Yes, seriously, Nick. Grow up!" Anna was back to school principal mode. "Neel, it's really important that we get enough time to check out all the rooms of the house. And I can't think of anything better. Can you?"

Neel had to admit that it seemed the best option, but he wasn't going to give in so easily. "I'm seven years old. Which grown-up will believe that I can't wait even a few minutes to get back home?"

"Hmm... that's a fair point," said Anna and started twirling her hair again.

Neel smiled, pleased to be let off the hook.

"I guess we'll have to say you have a stomach bug or diarrhea or something..." said Anna. The pillow, which had only just quieted down, started gurgling once again.

"Ann-naaaaa," wailed Neel.

"I'm sorry, Neel, but there is really no other choice. Just do this once and I'll buy you chocolate, okay? And Nick will play cricket with you forever."

"I don't want to play with Nick at all," said Neel. "But I don't mind the chocolate."

"Promise!" said Anna, pinching her neck. "Let's do it right now or it'll get to lunchtime and we'll miss the chance. Nick, go up and throw the ball into their side of the courtyard. Yell something so it sounds real. Then come to the front door. Neel and I will wait for you there!"

They put on their slippers and went their separate ways. Nick raced up to the roof, grabbing the ball on the way while Neel took the key and accompanied Anna downstairs. As they were approaching the front door, they heard a muffled yell from the roof, followed by a faint thudding.

Anna gave Neel a knowing wink. In a few moments, Nick had clattered down the stairs to join them.

"What's the commotion for?" asked Ma, calling out from one of the rooms above.

"It's okay. The silly boys have only knocked their ball into the tenant's house, haven't they? But don't worry. I'm going with them to sort it all out," said Anna.

The answer seemed to satisfy Ma. She said nothing more. The three let themselves out of the front door and went over to the tenant's entrance.

"Let me handle it," said Anna. She marched up to the door and pressed the buzzer. The three of them stepped back and waited.

"Who is it?" called out a voice from above them. A man leaned over from the balcony and squinted at them. "Who are you? What do you want? We don't want to buy anything." Without further notice, he did an about-face and disappeared back indoors.

"Oh-oh," said Nick, "that was sudden. Anna, we have to try again!"

Anna stepped up to the buzzer once again and pressed it. Standing back, she looked up. The man emerged again, annoyed.

"Look here, I don't want anything and I really don't like these kinds of pranks. Please go away."

Before he could make another move, Anna piped up, "Mr. Gupta, its Anna from next door. We aren't selling anything. We just need to get our ball back. It's fallen into your compound."

"Anna? Who's Anna?" he asked, screwing up his face and squinting at her even more. "Oh, Tapan's daughter? Why didn't you say so at the start? Wait just a second, I'll let you in."

The children waited for a few minutes until they heard shuffling sounds within come up to the door and latches and chains being opened. The door swung open. The man poked his head out of the door.

"Come in, come in," he said. "You've lost your ball you say?"

"Yes, Mr. Gupta," said Anna, "Is it okay if we come

in to look for it? Oh, and these are my cousins, Nick and Neel."

"Hello sir," the boys said in unison. Neel peered around the man in the hope of spotting a mysterious locked door.

"Come on. Come, take a look. Did it fall off the roof? I'm guessing it's in the courtyard."

The children filed into the house and into the courtyard, where they pretended to start looking for the ball. Nick spotted it almost instantly - it was lying bang in the middle of the space, in plain sight. He quickly kicked it behind a flowerpot.

"Neel, now," Nick muttered to Neel as they made their way to a corner of the courtyard.

Neel started feeling hot at the back of his neck. A little further away, he could see Anna's eyes boring into him. It was now or never.

"Mister..." he said and paused.

"Yes, little fellow?" said the man looking inquiringly at him.

"M-mister, I need to go to the bathroom," said Neel.

"Oh, sure, sure!" said the man. "It's upstairs. Come, let me show you the way."

"Oh, no, no, sir," Nick stepped in. Walking up to the man, he said in a conspiratorial whisper. "Actually... he's got an upset stomach. I think he needs to do the big job. He'll be too embarrassed to go with you. Is it okay if I take him?"

"Oh!" said the man taking a couple of quick steps away from Neel as if he were a bomb about to explode. "Yes, yes, please go ahead. The bathroom is one flight up and to your right."

The bathroom was right next to Nanima's room! What a stroke of luck!

"Come on, Neel. Hurry," said Nick as he hustled him up the stairs.

Behind him he heard Anna strike up a conversation, "So, Mr. Gupta, have you been reading about..." Nick smiled and shook his head in amazement. She was good at this. Who would have thought?

They had soon found the bathroom. Nick shoved Neel inside.

"But why do I have to go in?" Neel asked. "I want to help search for the door. It will be quicker if both of us do it."

"It's too dangerous," reasoned Nick. "What if someone comes to check? No. We need you in there. Groan a bit if anyone comes by."

Neel looked disgusted at the thought but turned towards the bathroom nonetheless. He fished out the key from his pocket, placed it in Nick's hand, and gingerly stepped through the door.

"Nick," he wailed. "The floor is all wet."

"Yeah, just walk on tiptoes. Remember to lock the door from inside," replied Nick, before pulling the door shut on him. He had no time to waste.

Peeping down from the corridor, he could see Anna and the man in conversation below. The ball was still where he had hidden it.

Stepping lightly, he tiptoed his way towards the room adjoining the staircase. This was definitely the room adjacent to Didu's room. This was Nanima's room. Hands shaking with excitement, he held out the key and reached for the lock on the door.

But the door was unlatched. There was no lock at all on it. He pushed on the door lightly and it swung open. Inside, he could make out the contours of a bed and a wardrobe. This was not a treasure-bearing strong room. It was just an ordinary bedroom.

Nick felt an emptiness in his stomach. The kind you get when an airplane starts its descent. Was there no secret, no mystery after all? Were the jewels actually stolen decades ago?

No. He had to believe that the note meant something - that there indeed was treasure hidden where *nobody would care*!

Maybe Nanima had more than one room?

Gathering himself, he rushed to try the key in the next room. It didn't work. Neither did the next. Both had the same bland modern locks. Nick panicked. He had tried all the rooms and yet nothing worked.

Maybe there was a secret door inside Nanima's room?

Throwing caution to the winds, he raced back to the room and pushed his way in. He gently shut the door and started looking around. There was a bed and a wardrobe. A dressing table and mirror stood against the wall. That seemed to be it. No doors anywhere..

Nick started trying the key on the dressing table drawers, which had keyholes but didn't fit the key. He knew it was futile, since the table couldn't have been more than a few years old.

His last bet was the wardrobe. Wooden and lightly carved it seemed to date back to when the house was built. Walking over, he pushed the key into the hole and started trying to turn it. It seemed to give a little, so he forced it a bit more.

Just then, he heard footsteps coming up the stairs.

"Hey, kid," called the man. "Are you okay? I didn't hear from you or Nick, so wanted to come and check."

The footsteps came up, passed Nanima's room and came to a halt around where the bathroom was.

"Hey, kid," the man knocked on the door. "Everything alright in there?"

Nick could hear some muffled sounds. They seemed to satisfy the man, who started walking back down the stairs. After a few steps, the footsteps stopped.

"Hey, where's Nick?" the man called out. Hearing nothing, he turned and started walking back up.

It would be a matter of seconds before the man burst through the door and found Nick. In a panic, Nick redoubled his efforts with the key, hoping against hope that it would turn out to be the right keyhole. It wouldn't turn any further.

Realizing it was hopeless, Nick started turning the key the other way so he could slip it out and leave, but it wouldn't turn back. It was stuck.

Outside, the man was calling Nick's name. He was getting closer to the door. Quick as a flash, Nick ducked and wriggled under the bed, leaving the key in the wardrobe as the door opened.

Oh please, please let him not spot the key - or me! prayed Nick, curling himself up into a ball at the far corner of the bed and holding his breath.

The man walked a few steps into the room and stopped. Nick could see his feet shifting as he turned this way and that.

Moments passed. It felt like Nick had been trapped under the bed for hours. He was starting to feel claustrophobic. He didn't know how much longer he could hold himself.

Finally, just as he was getting ready to burst out from under the bed and give himself up, the man made up his mind and walked away. He slowly stepped out of the room and Nick heard the clack of slippers making their way down the stairs.

Nick waited for a few more seconds to make sure he was completely safe. He wriggled out from under the bed and dashed to the wardrobe. The key was still there. He pulled at it, but it was firmly lodged in the keyhole. Desperate to get out of the room, Nick started wiggling the key up and down, back and forth, in an attempt to dislodge it.

He was deep in concentration when the door burst open behind him.

"Nick!"

Nick fell to his side, his hand still grasping the key, which came unstuck with a jerk. His ribs struck the bed frame hard.

Ignoring the pain, Nick leapt up, brandishing the key in front of him like a knife.

"What-? Who-?" he went, eyes wide open. Whoever it was, he would not go down without a fight. He would take down at least one or two assailants before they got him.

Neel stood before him, looking equally petrified. "What on earth are you doing?" he asked. "Stop fooling around and let's get out of here. I was sure that Mr. Gupta would catch you."

Nick just gaped at him. It took him a few moments to register what was happening. It wasn't an angry mob of tenants. It was Neel trying to get him back to safety.

"Okay," puffed Nick, still out of breath. He clutched his side. The fall had been a bad one.

They exited the room, closed the door and made their way down the stairs, where they found the man talking animatedly with Anna. She seemed to be trying to pacify him.

"... and Nick is not up there at all. Where could he have gone?" said the man, arms waving agitatedly in the air as they walked up to him. "One goes poop, the other goes poof? What is this? Tell me."

He would have gone on if Nick hadn't tapped him on his shoulder.

"Hi Mr. Gupta," he said smiling as if nothing had happened. He tried hard to ignore his throbbing rib.

The man stared at him like he was a genie or a ghost or something. "Where did you come from? I went up and looked everywhere for you, but you were gone."

"Sorry sir, I got bored waiting for Neel so I went to the roof to try and pluck a mango. You have such a nice mango tree. I would have asked you of course, before taking it home!"

The man stared at Nick. "Well, I called for you so many times. Why didn't you answer me?"

"Sorry, sorry. I didn't hear you..." said Nick, trying to think of a better excuse.

"Look uncle, there's the ball," Neel yelled, running over to pick it up and distracting the man, who turned around to look at Neel.

Thank you, Nick mouthed silently at him.

"Okay," said Anna. "That's that. Shall we leave now? Thank you so much Mr. Gupta for your help and for allowing Neel to use the bathroom. Neel, say thanks!"

“Thank you, Mister,” said Neel, stepping out onto the street.

“Thanks a lot, sir,” said Nick, stepping out behind him.

“See you later, Mr. Gupta,” said Anna, following the boys and turning around to shut the door.

Inside, the man was just standing still. He seemed to realize he’d been tricked, but didn’t know exactly how.

They closed the door and raced back to their house. Anna and Neel couldn’t wait to hear what Nick had found.

CHAPTER 9

Flash of Inspiration

"Nothing? You found nothing?"

Neel threw up his hands in exasperation. How could he not have found something? The note clearly stated the treasure was in Nanima's room. Was he blind or something?

"Did you check the room properly? Or were you just hiding under the bed the entire time?" asked Neel, sarcastically.

"Maybe there was nothing to find?" Anna chimed in. "Perhaps this was just a really old prank that happened to find its mark, like, fifty years too late?" She giggled, despite herself.

Neel turned on her with a look that wiped the grin right off her face. "What do *you* care? You just showed up and barged into our mystery! Fat lot of help you provided, with your bright idea of having me sit on the toilet for hours. We'd have been better off with Nick on the potty and me doing the hunting!"

Neel threw himself face first onto the bed. "It's all over."

Nick's face went red. He slumped into a chair and pulled his knees up to his chest.

Anna tried to console the two. "Look, at least you had fun trying to solve this mystery, right? Think of how bored you'd have been otherwise."

There was no response. Anna walked out of the room.

A few minutes passed. Neel lay on his back, silently staring at the ceiling. The streaks of dirt on his face the only indication that he had been sobbing. Nick had his chin on his knees, staring into space, lost in his own thoughts.

Anna came back into the room.

"Is everyone feeling better now that you've had a good cry?"

"I-did-not-cry," said Nick between clenched teeth. Neel kept gazing at the ceiling.

"Okay," continued Anna, as if everything were normal. "Look what I have."

She thrust one book into Nick's hand and balanced another on Neel's tummy.

Nick looked up at her, puzzled. She never handed out books willingly. You had to beg her for hours until she grudgingly parted with even a brochure. And this one was a thick tome, leather bound with gold lettering on the cover.

"The Adventures of Narnia," he read aloud, glancing at the cover. "Wow, *The Lion, the Witch and the Wardrobe*!" He'd been asking to borrow this for the last two summers, with zero success. What a windfall! He eagerly flipped the pages till he got to the beginning of the first chapter.

"Careful, careful!" cautioned Anna. The book had once belonged to Dadu, and she'd kept it very carefully, reading it bit by bit over weeks so it didn't get spoilt. The pages were brittle. She didn't want her clumsy brother to tear them off with his fumbling!

Neel was looking a great deal happier too. He had *Red Rackham's Treasure,* the Tintin comic with a shark-shaped submarine on the cover. With a cover like that, how could the story not be good! He wiped his face with the end of his t-shirt. This would be almost as much fun as finding the real treasure. Placing the book on the bed, he flipped over, propped up his head on his hands and began to read.

Anna arranged her things at the writing table. She wanted to get a head start on the following term's math chapters. She looked back at the two lost in their respective fantasy worlds and smiled, "Books... they never fail." Turning back, she busied herself in her textbooks. Her head bowed, she began to write out notes.

Silence fell on the room. They forgot about their troubles. Minutes turned into half an hour, and then an hour.

"Poof!" said Neel, flipping over the last page and slapping the book closed. "That was every bit as amazing as I thought it would be. Anna, can I get another Tintin?"

Anna, lost in her studies, grunted.

"I guess that means no," said Neel pleasantly. One Tintin was already one more than he could have expected.

He looked at the clock. It was just past two in the afternoon. It would be hours before snack time. There was nothing to do till then. He had three options - sleep, get bored or bother someone. The choice was obvious.

"What are you reading, Nick?" he asked. "That book looks super-boring!"

"Mmm?" said Nick, paying no attention to Neel.

"I said it looks boring."

"Hmm? Boring? No, it's not boring, it's amazing," said Nick, who was by now midway through the book and didn't want to be distracted.

"What's it called?"

"Huh? Just read the name. It's on the cover."

"Can't read it. It's all some funny writing, all loopy."

"It's old English script, Neel," said Anna from her corner. "Very old books had writing like that. The book is called 'The Chronicles of Narnia'."

"The Conicals of Nannia? Who's Nannia?" persisted Neel.

"Not who, what," said Anna. "It's the Chronicles – stories – of Narnia, not Nannia. Narnia is a magical place with talking creatures and wicked witches and whatnot."

"Just read the blurb, Neel," snapped Nick, "And don't bother us. I know what you're doing. Go find someone else to bother."

"But Nick."

"What?"

"There's no blurb," said Neel innocently. He wondered how long he could keep this up till Nick snapped.

Nick slammed the book shut to point out the blurb to Neel, but no words came out. There was no blurb. Nick deflated. Of course this one had no blurb. It was leather bound. The blurb would be inside.

"Okay, yeah, so the blurb is inside," he said scratching his neck, while Neel continued to look at him innocently.

"Look, Nilu, I'll read out the blurb, but please don't bother me anymore. I've wanted to read this book for years and I won't get another chance unless we ask Ma to buy it for me. And that would be a big waste since Anna already has the book. I'd rather have her buy me something new. Please don't be a pest. Okay?"

Neel nodded. Maybe he'd let Nick be, or maybe he wouldn't. He'd play it by ear. He was feeling feisty.

Turning to the back of the book, Nick read out aloud, "Four adventurers step through a wardrobe door and into the land of Narnia -- a land enslaved by the power of the White Witch. But when almost all hope is lost, the return of the Great Lion, Aslan, signals a great change... and a great sacrifice."

He looked at Neel. "Okay? That's it. That's the story."

He was about to settle back into the chair when Neel said, "Nick, what's the meaning of the word 'enslaved'? I can't understand the story unless I know the meaning."

"God. You're such a brat. Enslaved means held captive, like holding someone as a slave."

"Oh, okay, got it."

"Thank you." Nick settled back in his chair and found the passage he was reading. In moments he had been transported back to a faraway land, where…

"Nick, how did they make their way through a wardrobe? I mean, wouldn't they have bumped into the back of it?" said Neel.

"What do you mean? They just did. Why are you bothering me like this?"

"I mean, did they chop down the back of the wardrobe or something?"

"Neel, it's just a fantasy story. It's magic. There are, like, witches and talking lions and everything. And you're worried about how they got through the wardrobe? Seriously?"

"Anna," he called out. "Anna please could you give him another book? *Please* or he'll never stop talking!"

Anna shushed him. She was in the middle of a complicated trigonometric problem.

"Great, *now* you go back to being your usual self. Couldn't you have stayed fun Anna for just a few more hours?" grumbled Nick.

"So, Nick," went Neel. "How did they enter Narnia then?"

Nick busied himself in the pages of the book. He flipped a page loudly.

Unfazed, Neel trotted over to Nick and bent down by his ear. "Nik ki nik ki nik ki nik ki," he went in a sing-song voice like an annoying ambulance siren.

"Why you-" roared Nick, half-springing out of his chair. The heavy book fell to the floor with a thud, pages flying.

Neel fell backwards to the floor, throwing his arms up to protect his face. Dropping her pen, Anna threw back her chair and bounded over to block the blow. Reaching out with both hands, she took a firm grasp of Nick's arm and wrestled him back. Neel took the opportunity to scramble into a corner.

"What on earth-?" yelped Nick, flailing his arms and struggling unsuccessfully to get out of her grasp. "Don't - push - me!"

"Don't you dare hit Neel," Anna gasped, trying to wrestle him down onto the chair and keep a hold of her glasses at the same time.

"Peace, peace," said Nick, after a few moments. It had been years since he and Anna had had a fight like this one. She had been tough back then and she was more than a match for him now. He dropped his shoulders and Anna took the opportunity to shove him back into the chair. Nick just lay there, panting.

Sensing his opportunity, Neel sprang up and hid behind Anna, his arms encircling her waist.

"And you, Neel," said Anna turning to shoot Neel a dark look. "You really need to stop annoying Nick – *and* me.

As she said this, her eyes fell on the book, now lying spread-eagled on the ground. A few pages seemed to have come loose.

"Nick!" she cried out, her hand flying to her mouth. "What have you done? This was Dadu's book!"

She knelt next to it and started gathering up the pages. She picked up the book, checked the binding to make sure it hadn't come apart and tucked the pages in before closing it.

Turning to Nick, she said, "I knew I-".

And then Anna's expression changed. Her face went slack. Nick saw her eyes suddenly unfocus. She turned to the book and gazed at it, mouth slightly agape, a frown beginning to form.

Nick and Neel looked at each other.

"This is it," said Neel. "We've broken Anna. She's lost her mind. Soon she'll be checked into an asylum and Mesho and Mashi will have nobody to look after them when they're old."

A thought struck Neel. "Does this mean we can take her books?"

Anna came to with a start.

"No," she said firmly to Neel. "Nick, I think I have it. I think I've found the answer to your riddle!"

"Oh, no, here we go again," said Neel.

"No, listen. I *do* have the answer. It's in the book!"

Now it was Nick's turn to doubt Anna's sanity. "So..." he said, "the answer to the riddle about a treasure in this house is written in this book? Mr. C.S. Lewis was personally involved in hiding our family jewels?"

He rolled his eyes and looked over at Neel, who was looking skywards and whistling as he twirled a finger at his temple.

"No, you silly people," grumbled Anna. "Hang on, I'll show you what I mean. Nick, where's the note and all the photocopies you made?"

Puzzled but curious, Nick walked over to the desk and brought out the note and the photocopies.

"Could you get me your notebook and a pen as well please?" said Anna.

Nick handed everything over to Anna, who spread them out on the bed and motioned for Nick and Neel to come over.

"Look at the note. What does this line say?" She pointed to the last line of the note.

"Behind Nanima's door," said Neel, barely looking at the note. "The room Nick didn't search, remember?"

He shot a glance at Nick.

"No, wait, look more closely. Look at the photocopy. Do you see how the word 'Nanima' is written all loopily?" said Anna, placing the copy in the middle so all three could get a closer look.

"Yes, it's all loopy - like you're sounding right now!" said Neel, smirking at Anna.

"Doesn't it look like the writing on the cover of the book?" said Anna, now placing the book next to the papers.

"Hm, yes it kind of does," said Nick.

"Does the note really say Nanima?" asked Anna.

Anna started writing something just below the word Nanima on the copy Nick had written out in his notebook.

"Hey," interjected Nick. "Don't spoil it."

"Calm down," said Anna, still writing slowly. It took a few seconds, as she took breaks to check the writing on the cover of the book.

"Voila!" she exclaimed when she was done. "What does it say?"

Nick and Neel crowded closer to the notebook. What was Anna trying to do? She seemed to have written the same thing, just in that funny handwriting.

"It says Nanima," said Nick, puzzled. "What else would it say?"

"Look closely, young Padawan," said Anna. "Or does it instead say-" Anna carefully over-wrote the word. "-Narnia!" she ended with a flourish.

Narnia

You could have heard a pin drop. Nick picked up the photocopy to check the original handwriting. Now that he saw it, it did indeed say Narnia. He looked at the note in awe.

"But what does this mean?" asked Nick, looking up from the paper to Anna and Neel in confusion. "How can something be hidden behind Narnia's door? Narnia is a fantasy world. It's not real." He looked down, half-expecting Mr. Tumnus, the Faun, to crawl out from under the bed.

"True," said Anna, grinning. "But what is Narnia's door?"

"A wardrobe!" shrieked Neel, who had been silent till now. "The wardrobe they have to pass through to get to Narnia!"

"Full marks, little Nilu," said Anna patting her cousin on the back. "You do have brains after all. The *jewels we adore* are somehow hidden in a wardrobe. So where might that wardrobe be?"

As one, all three of them turned to the far wall. Right in the middle of the wall was a pair of built-in wooden doors. It was the closet where Mashi kept all the woolens and bedclothes.

"Neel, could you please bring the key?" asked Anna, as calmly as she could.

Neel nodded and went to get it while Anna swung open the doors.

"But Anna, this closet is always open. There's never been anything inside other than these clothes and a musty smell!" said Neel handing the key over.

"Neel, like you said, the secret of the wardrobe was always about how they got to the other side, not about the doors of the wardrobe. There must be a secret compartment in here that can only be opened with the key. We have to empty out the wardrobe to find it. Here, give me a hand."

Anna started lifting out the neatly stowed bundles of sheets and clothing and handing them over to Nick and Neel, who placed them on the bed. In a few minutes, the closet had been emptied and the three of them pressed up against the opening.

CHAPTER 10

Mystery Revealed

"There's definitely something there. It's hollow," said Nick knocking on the wooden back of the closet. "But I can't find a way to open it."

"Neither can I," said Anna, who had been examining the edges of the closet with her fingernails. She couldn't find even a crack.

"Can we just break it down?" asked Neel hopping up and down. He was ready to butt the closet with his head, if that's what it took to get to the treasure.

"No. The wood looks pretty solid," said Nick. "Our mystery person wouldn't have wanted to make the opening that obvious or the secret would have been easily revealed. The key is tiny, perhaps the keyhole is tough to see. Neel, get the flashlight."

Neel raced off while Nick and Anna continued to look for any kind of mark.

Neel was soon back, empty-handed. "Nick. The flashlight is gone. I think someone kept it away. What do we do now?"

This was a problem. Nick didn't want to ask someone for the flashlight. They were too close to solving the mystery. On the other hand, they couldn't very well just keep banging away at the wall with their fists. Neel looked like he was about to burst.

"Nick, did you ever check to see if the old flashlight works?" asked Anna. "If it does, we could just use that. We probably have new batteries in the kitchen."

"No, we didn't," said Nick. "That's an idea. Could you get us two batteries? Size D."

He walked over to fetch the flashlight while Anna returned from the kitchen.

"Here you go," said Anna, holding out two red batteries.

Nick dropped them into the battery chamber one by one. Unlike the first time, they went in easily. Nick smiled at the memory. It seemed so long ago now!

He closed the battery compartment and pressed the switch. It came on with a powerful glow.

"Hooray, it works!" squealed Neel.

Nick pointed the light at the closet, where it lit up a bright rectangular area.

"Odd, said Nick. "Flashlights usually throw out round beams. And this one has a round face as well. Why is the beam rectangular? Is this how old flashlights used to work?" He switched off the light and started examining it.

"It doesn't matter, Nick," squeaked Neel. "Stop fussing about things so much. Just move the beam around and we'll be able to see everything."

"Calm down, Neel. The treasure has been here for like fifty years, a few more minutes won't do it any harm."

He had a careful look at the bulb. It was round. There didn't seem to be any marks on it. The glass and the mirror inside, on the other hand, were badly damaged. The top and bottom were scuffed. But the rest of the surface was unmarked, almost looked new. In fact, the damage was weirdly symmetrical. It was almost like someone had scratched them with a sharp object.

Wait. *Had* someone scuffed up the glass? Had they meant to make a rectangular shaped beam? Why?

Nick was struck by a thought. "Anna, do you have a magnifying glass by any chance?" he asked.

"Magnifying glass? No. Why do you want one?" she asked.

"Oh, I just wanted to check something on this glass," he said, holding the flashlight up close to his eyes. "Is there anything at all that might be able to magnify things?"

"Well, I have my glasses. They're for reading so they aren't going to magnify it a lot."

"Nice," said Nick, holding out his hand for the glasses.

He placed the flashlight on its end, closed one eye and peered at the flashlight through the glasses. His eyes felt weird looking through them. He hoped they wouldn't get spoilt.

He found it almost immediately. A little black dot on the glass. It looked like it had been carefully placed there..

Nick stood up. The last piece of the puzzle had just fallen into place.

"Neel," he said in a quiet voice. "Please hold the flashlight and point it at the closet."

Neel, eager to be finally doing something, held up the flashlight and switched it on. The beam lit up the closet once again, with the rectangle projecting at an angle.

"No, not that way, Neel," said Nick. "Rotate the flashlight so the rectangle lines up with the edges of the closet."

Neel dutifully adjusted the beam, which now illuminated the closet fully and some of the wall.

"Okay, now move closer, so the rectangle fits exactly on the edges of the closet."

"Niiiick…" whined Neel.

"Just do it, Neel, you'll soon figure out why we need to do this. Do you want to find the treasure or not?"

Neel shuffled a few steps forward to make the rectangle fit. "Happy?"

"Very happy," said Nick. "Just stay there and don't move. Anna, would you mind bringing over the pen and standing to the left of the closet?"

Anna took up her position and stood, pen in hand, looking quizzically at Nick. This was all looking crazy but she'd learnt to trust Nick's detective instincts.

"Okay," said Nick. "Can you see that little black blob-like shadow towards the right of the opening?"

Neel stepped in to try and see. The flashlight wobbled in his hands.

"No, no. Stay where you were, Neel. Just stay where you were," ordered Nick. "Make sure the rectangle lines up like before. The position of the blob is very important."

Neel did as he was told and re-positioned the light.

"Anna, could you draw a circle around the blob?" asked Nick.

Taking care not to block the blob with her own shadow, Anna carefully traced out a circle around its edges.

"Okay, Neel, good job. You're done now. You can switch off the light."

Neel flicked the switch off and came over.

"What was all that?" asked Anna.

"Hang on, hang on, we still have a treasure to find," said Nick. "Anna, may I trouble you once again?"

"I suppose."

"Try to use the tip of that pen you're holding to scratch away near the center of the circle."

"Nick."

"What?"

"You're turning into a pompous brat," said Anna, annoyed, but curious.

Anna went forward and scratched around the circle, starting in the middle and then expanding out in a spiral so she didn't miss anything.

"Oh!" she said, as the tip of the pen suddenly fell through a little opening. "There's a hole here."

"Exactly," said Nick, his eyes shining. "Neel, here, take the key. Try pushing it into the hole. I think you'll find it's a perfect fit."

Neel grabbed the key and was at the closet in a hop and a skip. He slid the key into the hole and turned it.

Click.

Trrch. The edge of the closet fell forward a few millimeters. Nick was right. This was the secret door.

Neel started tugging at the closet, but his hands slipped off the edges. Nick and Anna rushed forward to help him.

"Anna, you're the tallest. Grab the upper edge. Neel, take the lower edge. I'll pull on a shelf," said Nick. "Ready? One… two… Heave!"

The door groaned but didn't move any further.

"Again. One… two… Heeeave!" yelled Nick.

The three pulled with all their strength. *Trrrrch.* The closet swung open a few inches, revealing a dark space about three feet high.

"Okay, we can hold on better now," puffed Nick. "I'll pull on the middle section. Anna, you and Neel take the top and bottom like before."

"One more," called Nick. "One… two... Heave!"

Trrrrrrk. The door swung open.

"Quick, the flashlight," called Nick.

Neel grabbed it and shone the light into the space. Nick and Anna knelt down next to him and peered inside.

It was a small space, just a couple of feet deep. Within it, lying on its side, was a wooden chest! Years of humidity had taken its toll on the wood, though it still seemed sturdy.

"Get it out," said Neel.

Nick began to reach in, but stopped and drew his hand back. God knows what creepy-crawlies were behind or maybe even in the box. Perhaps there were cockroaches. What if they were the flying variety? He shuddered.

Finding a foot-long wooden ruler that was lying on the desk, he poked at the box, squatting as far from the opening as he could.

"What are you doing?" asked Anna.

"Oh, er, I just wanted to check if the wood was sturdy enough. After all it is pretty old and damaged."

"Oh, yeah, good point," said Anna, nodding in agreement.

Nick tapped at the chest a few more times.

"Shouldn't you move a bit closer so you can hit it harder?" asked Anna.

Nick thought he heard a scuttling sound from somewhere in the shadows.

"Eh... oh no this is alright, I think," said Nick, dropping the ruler and standing up in one smooth move. "N-Neel, since you're the one who began this mystery, I think you should have the honor of bringing out the chest. It's all right, I've tested the wood thoroughly."

"Really, Nick?" asked Neel, looking up at him. His eyes lit up.

"Really," said Nick, grinning back at him. He took the flashlight from his brother and trained it on the opening.

Neel sat down and grabbed at the chest with both hands. Hooking his arm on the inside surface, he leaned back and pulled as hard as he could. The chest slid out a few inches, making a groaning sound as it scraped over the rough floor of its enclosure. Nick, half expecting an entire Jurassic Park to pour out of the hole, took a couple of steps back until he fell back on the writing table. He continued to keep the flashlight beam fixed on the opening.

"Wow, the chest looks heavy," said Anna.

She leaned over to help Neel bring it out. Half-dragging, half-lifting the box, the two cousins brought it out onto the middle of the room.

"Hey, Nick, the box is here. You can stop lighting up the hole now," said Anna, wondering whether Nick was expecting there to be another chest.

"Oh, yeah. I was just checking to make sure everything was in order," said Nick, taking one last look to make sure the hole was one hundred percent insect free before switching off the flashlight and placing it on the table.

The three knelt over the box, looking at it in awe. Even in its worn-out condition, they could tell that it was beautifully made. It had the rich, honey-like glow of really old wood. Its surface was inlaid with fine patterns of metal and the lid was held closed by a simple latch without a lock. The mystery man had clearly decided that the riddles had been enough, there was no further need to lock it.

"Neel," said Nick quietly. "Go for it. This is your moment."

Neel slowly lifted the latch. His mind filled up with so many images - playing cricket, wiggling under the bed to find the ball, finding the note, the photocopy shop, the hunt for the right lock, finding the keyhole in the wardrobe... And now, he, Nick and Anna were about to reveal the family treasure. Was this really happening?

It was too much for him. He screwed his eyes tightly shut and lifted the lid in one quick motion, letting it drop to the ground with a thud. He heard gasps from Nick and Anna. He couldn't bear to look. Was there treasure inside? Or was this a prank after all, with a note inside gloating over how well they had been fooled? Was there anything at all? For a few moments, the world came to a standstill. No sights, no sounds, nothing but the delicious feeling of anticipation.

He opened his eyes a crack and peeked down. He could see the hazy outlines of two pairs of hands. Something was glittering. Something that looked like things he had only seen in comics before.

He opened his eyes fully and the world came back to life.

"Oh my God!" Anna was screaming over and over. She was on her knees, her body swaying wildly back and forth like some sort of spirit had possessed her.

"We did it, we did it, we did it," Nick was singing as he skipped and pranced around the room.

It was indeed treasure. Heaps of it. More than he had imagined. More than Red Rackham's treasure even.

There were necklaces and bracelets and earrings and coins and cufflinks. There was gold and silver and diamonds. There were beautiful little images of Hindu gods. There was everything you can think of when you hear the word 'treasure'.

"Oh my God - the peacock earrings!" rasped Anna. She sounded like she was choking. "Nick, Neel, remember the earrings Didu told us about? The ones Nanima used to wear? They're not lost. They're here! They've been here all these years…!"

Neel didn't say a word. Not while Anna yelled herself hoarse. Not while Nick nearly squashed him as he hopped about the room. Not even when Ma and Baba and Mashi and Mesho came rushing up the steps to find out what had happened.

He just sat there, cross-legged in front of the treasure. The treasure that he had helped find. He closed his eyes again.

It wasn't a dream.

But, in a way, it was!

***

Hours later, the room had been cleared of boxes and treasure and people. Explanations had been made. The grown-ups had gone away to discuss the events and decide what to do with the treasure.

Anna and Nick returned to put the closet back in its place. They were still discussing their adventure when Anna noticed the book lying forgotten on the bed. She scooped it up.

"Nick, you got away easy this time," she exclaimed. "How many times have I told you to be careful with my books? You ripped the pages on this one!"

"Yeah," said Nick. "But I figured this wasn't really *your* book..."

Anna stared at him for a second. Then they both burst out laughing.

CHAPTER 11

A Noble Cause

It had been a week since the discovery. A lot had happened. The treasure had been carefully itemized and evaluated by a jeweler as well as a historian. The jeweler had estimated a value that far surpassed the expectations of anyone in the family.

The historian had agreed about the monetary value of the treasure. However, he had also stressed the historic value of the items. Much had been lost, looted or sold from old Kolkata mansions over the years and it was extremely rare to come across an intact family collection like this one.

The kids had been invited to a long family conference, where it had eventually been decided that the treasure should be donated to a museum for safekeeping and for the enjoyment and benefit of society. Left to themselves, the grown-ups might have been tempted to keep the jewels, but the children had been firmly in favor of the museum. And Didu had helped swing the vote by pointing out that the children should get to choose since they were the ones who had found the treasure!

As a concession to Ma and Mashi, it was agreed that each child would get to keep one item as a memento of their extraordinary adventure. Anna, who had secretly desired them all along, got to keep the peacock earrings. She promised to lend them to Ma whenever she had to attend a fancy work event or wedding. Nick picked out a coin that dated back to the late 1800s for its "historic value" and Neel chose a gold medallion because he felt he deserved a medal for his heroism.

It had taken a few days to arrange the transfer of the valuables to the museum. An armored car with four hefty-looking guards had come to pick up the valuables, which they had moved from the chest to a heavy metal suitcase with three combination locks.

"Lucky the treasure had not been in a box like that one or we'd never have got it open," joked Neel, as they loaded the suitcase into the vehicle. The others laughed.

As news of the discovery spread, the local press had come calling. Nick, Neel and Anna had been invited to give interviews about the discovery to various newspapers. They had even come on local TV.

In a few short days, Anna had become a local celebrity. So many of her school friends called to hear the story that Mesho had to switch off his phone at night or none of them would get any sleep! The Sunday supplement even ran a profile piece titled 'Anna-lytical' with a photo of Anna in full school uniform sitting at her study table and frowning hard at Stephen Hawking's *A Brief History of Time.* It was captioned *The future of our country.*

Anna had spent the entire day walking on tip-toe and red-carpet waving at family members. She even tried to get Nick to take a photo of her waving at an imaginary crowd.

***

For once, everyone was at home at the same time. With all the press and autograph hunters milling about outside, it had been difficult for anyone to leave home anyway and a family lunch was deemed a fitting way to close out the week.

"So, Nick, with all the craziness over the past few days, I forgot to ask you earlier," said Ma, "How did you figure out the flashlight thing? What made you realize it had to be pointed in a certain way?"

"Hah!" said Nick, still proud of himself for figuring out that clue. Along with the photocopier, that had also been a shining moment.

"We knew that our mystery person couldn't just have put a keyhole in plain sight. He had to have hidden it in a way that only he or she could find it. That's where the old flashlight came into the picture. It wasn't just a hiding place for the note, it was also a means to find the keyhole. I realized that the light beam wasn't rectangular by accident; it was carefully made that way by someone who had rubbed out the flashlight's mirroring. When I realized that, I figured the rectangle had to fit the door, which meant they must have marked the location of the keyhole on the mirror as well. Everything else was obvious."

"Amazing," said Ma. She was proud of her children, not just for solving the mystery but for doing it together. Even to the press Nick had given a lot of the credit to Neel, which she thought was a very nice gesture on his part. She beamed at him from across the table.

"But Nick," said Mesho chewing a mouthful of rice, "you know you're still missing one part of the mystery."

"What?" asked Nick and Neel, together.

"You remember that 'Mrs.' who wrote the note? You never figured out what that was."

"Oh... yeah," said Nick. In all the excitement, he'd forgotten completely about the mysterious writer.

"I have a theory," said Mesho.

"You do? What?"

"I think it was Sushobha Sen - Nanima. After all they were her jewels hidden in her room."

"I did think of that, Mesho. But why say 'these jewels she adores' if she's referring to herself?" said Nick. "And it would also be weird to sign off as Mrs., wouldn't it? Why not write a name of some sort, even if fake? Why sign off at all? She could have easily left the note anonymous."

"It wasn't even Mrs.," said Neel casually. "It was MRS, all in capital letters. Also, is anyone having that?" he asked, pointing to the last piece of fish.

"Oh, yes," said Nick, "I totally missed that. I wonder why she would write it that way." His words trailed off and he pinched his lip. It *was* strange.

"Guess not." Neel dragged the bowl over and overturned its contents onto his plate.

"But anyway," Nick resumed. "It doesn't really help us, does it? Capital or small, we don't have any clue who the mystery lady was."

"Unless-" Anna interjected. She had been twirling her hair. "Unless they were initials. All capitals would typically mean initials, wouldn't they? M.R.S, not Mrs. And M.R.S. could only refer to one person-"

"Manas Ranjan Sen!" cried Nick and Neel together.

"Oh my God," said Ma. "My grandfather was behind all this? He hid the treasure?"

"It makes sense, doesn't it?" said Anna. "They were his wife's jewels. Who else would know more about the house than the person who built it? I bet he made that hiding place right at the start, knowing that it could come in handy one day."

Nick nodded. It made sense.

Didu spoke up. "Nanima died in 1956. She was bedridden in her last few years and never put on her jewelry or nice clothes or anything. She just lived in her plain cotton saris till the day she died. After she was gone we went through all her belongings but never found the jewelry. We all thought they had been stolen. Back then there always used to be people around the house - visitors, workers, people selling stuff. We just assumed someone had crept in and taken them. But it was all here all the time, right in front of us."

She fell silent, trying to imagine the moment when Manas Ranjan had carefully packed all his wife's jewelry into a box and hidden it behind the closet. Did he mean to keep it hidden for all these years? Or had he planned to bring it out sometime later? That was one puzzle they would never be able to solve.

Didu gave a little sniff. As one, Nick, Neel and Anna got up and rushed over to console her.

"Group hug!" yelled Neel and they gave her a tight squeeze. The family smiled at them. Ma's eyes filled up with tears as she fumbled for her phone to take a photo.

Didu closed her eyes and gave in to their tight embrace. Wherever they were, she felt as though Manas Ranjan and his Nanima were standing side by side right now, looking down at this little family.

She knew they were smiling.

THE END

COMING SOON
The Ghost of Golconda

The Sen kids are in Hyderabad to attend the 500-year celebrations of Golconda Fort. But things go awry when a priceless artifact is stolen and reports emerge of ghostly music playing at the ancient citadel!

Why did the thief leave behind all the jewelry?
What made the spirits of the Golconda royals return?
And will Nick gather the courage to uncover their spooky secrets?

Made in the USA
Middletown, DE
15 December 2018